# THE
# *Allure*
# OF A
# THUG
# 2

A NOVEL BY

# NATISHA RAYNOR

*© 2019 Royalty Publishing House*

*Published by Royalty Publishing House*
*www.royaltypublishinghouse.com*

**ALL RIGHTS RESERVED**

Any unauthorized reprint or use of the material is prohibited. No part of this book may be reproduced or transmitted in any form or by any means, electronic or mechanical, including photocopying, recording, or by any information storage without express permission by the author or publisher. This is an original work of fiction. Names, characters, places and incidents are either products of the author's imagination or are used fictitiously and any resemblance to actual persons, living or dead, is entirely coincidental.

**Contains explicit language & adult themes suitable for ages 16+ only.**

**Royalty Publishing House** is now accepting manuscripts from aspiring or experienced urban romance authors!

## WHAT MAY PLACE YOU ABOVE THE REST:

Heroes who are the ultimate book bae: strong-willed, maybe a little rough around the edges but willing to risk it all for the woman he loves.

Heroines who are the ultimate match: the girl next door type, not perfect - has her faults but is still a decent person. One who is willing to risk it all for the man she loves.

The rest is up to you! Just be creative, think out of the box, keep it sexy and intriguing!

If you'd like to join the Royal family, send us the first 15K words (60 pages) of your completed manuscript to submissions@royaltypublishinghouse.com

# SYNOPSIS

Quadim realizes that Castillo made a grave mistake when his people didn't make sure Quadim was dead before getting rid of the body. Panama has a newfound vendetta against Quadim and he no longer cares about being on probation or going back to prison. His only thought is avenging what happened to his soulmate. Natalia meets a man that satisfies her desire to be loved by a thug. He's everything that Leonard isn't and Natalia soon learns that the grass is pretty much never greener on the other side. She wanted adventure, and she got it in Jovaughn, a handsome hustler with an abundance of money and a plethora of women. In the end, she realizes she may have bitten off more than she could chew.

# PREVIOUSLY....

## QUADIM

"Man what is you crying for? Shut the fuck up!" I barked at Quashon and immediately regretted it.

A nigga was fucked up. Castillo, Panama, and Diesel's bitch ass thought they killed me. Funny how Castillo talked about my team moving sloppy, and they didn't even make sure that I was dead for real before they left my body. Don't get it twisted, I damn near died. When a white lady out jogging found me tossed on the side of the road like trash, she couldn't even find a pulse. She thought I was dead. I didn't remember any of that, and I only knew it because the doctor told me. He and a few nurses told me more than once how lucky I was to be alive.

I told Quashon not to tell anybody that I was alive. Aside from him, Lynn, and my right-hand man Tony, no one knew anything about me. As far as they knew, I just dropped off the face of the Earth, and that's how I wanted it to stay until I got well enough to show my face. it was my first day out of the hospital and even though I could barely walk, I wanted Alex's ass. I wanted her worse than I wanted Castillo and Panama. Castillo would be hard to get because he was so powerful and connected. Alex was the easiest, so I started with that hoe.

It only took a few seconds to spray her ass with bullets, but even that took a lot out of me. I was out of breath and in pain when I got back to Lynn's crib. "You said you wanted to talk to her. Why did you shoot her? Is she dead?" he cried like a little bitch.

"Man fuck that hoe!" Once again, I regretted yelling as pain radiated through my body. My nostrils flared, and my chest heaved up and down as I waited for the pain to subside. It would probably be another month before I was back all the way one hundred. "She's the fucking opps! She supposed to love me, but she already laid up with the next nigga," I stated between clenched teeth while Lynn looked like she was about to cry. Both of their punk asses were pissing me off. "That bitch ass hoe ain't for me. She not loyal. She laid up with a nigga that left me for dead. You think I'm letting that shit ride?" I glared at him, but he didn't answer me.

My upper lip curled into a snarl when I saw snot dripping from his nose. "Lil' nigga go clean yourself up. Quit all that crying before I beat yo' ass. Had they really killed me, you'd be in foster care somewhere, and you want to cry over that hoe. Fuck outta here," I seethed.

Alex hadn't pulled the trigger. Alex hadn't left me for dead, but she still violated. I told her she was mine forever, and she must have thought a nigga was playing. If I couldn't have her, then nobody would, and it was just that simple.

"What now?" Lynn asked in a shaky voice.

I glared at her. "I stay here, and I get well. Then muhfuckas gon' feel me. If I come at Castillo while niggas think I'm dead, the better it will be for me. Even with him thinking I'm dead I still have to be careful and very calculated. That nigga doesn't take a shit without security. First, I knock his ass off and then I get that bitch ass Panama." A sadistic grin slid across my face. "That one is going to be special. I want to watch that nigga suffer. I'm going to make sure his death is real brutal and disrespectful, and then they can bury him next to his bitch."

# PANAMA

"Nigga when did you start smoking weed?" I laughed as I looked at Jay in amazement. Nigga was sitting across from me on his Italian leather sofa in a three-piece suit that looked like it cost a grip, smoking some of the finest kush. The potent smell had my mouth watering.

He laughed too. "My second year in law school. I started smoking more than Bob Marley." He shook his head at the memory. "Man, not on no gay shit, but I thought about you a lot over the years. Especially when I heard about a kid committing suicide from being bullied because that was almost me. Before you became my friend, I dead ass contemplated suicide several times. You kept kids off my ass, and I can never repay you for that. But I can try."

He passed me the blunt, and I took it. "I was just doing what was right. I ain't looking for no thanks." Even with my pops being in Panama, he still sent my mom money for me. My mom always worked and tried her best, so even though I wore fly shit and was a popular nigga, I just wasn't the type to pick on others.

Jay was a lil' fat, nerdy nigga. His people had money, but they weren't the type to buy him name brand clothes and shoes. They were on that you go to school to learn shit, and that got him picked on. One day our teacher teamed me up with him on a project, and I realized that he was a smart dude and cool. After that, no one could pick on him in my presence. After a while, niggas left him alone even when I wasn't around, 'cus they respected me just that much. I hadn't seen him since graduation, but I ran into him at the corner store, and I was shocked when he invited me back to his condo to smoke and shit. Dude was a lawyer and living nice as fuck.

"Well I'm telling you that you saved my life, and I got you. Anything you need. If you get a traffic ticket, I got you. I don't care what you need. Call me. I done slimmed down, started getting money, I dress better, life is good, but I still feel like I owe you."

I chuckled. "Aye, I'm not going to argue with having a lawyer in my pocket." My phone rang, and I looked at the screen. It was that time of the night where if a nigga wasn't trying to spend $1,000 or better, calls were getting ignored because I was off the clock. I saw that it was Butta though, so I answered. "What up fam?"

"I hate to be calling you with this bruh, but you might want to get to calling different hospitals." Butta's voice was solemn. "I heard Alex was laid out on the block. Somebody shot her up bruh."

It felt as if the wind had been knocked out of me. I heard him loud and clear, but what he said was such bullshit that I couldn't process it. I stood up with a million thoughts racing through my mind. "Butta are you sure?" my voice boomed.

"Yeah. It was at the house she used to live at with Quadim. Niggas heard gunshots, they went outside, and she was laid out on the sidewalk. I don't know where the ambulance took her, but the closest hospital would have been Rex."

My heart slammed into my chest. "A'ight bruh." I ended the call and had to damn near fight back tears. Who in the hell would have shot

Alex up? Why was she at the spot where she used to live with Quadim? That fuck nigga was dead. Wasn't he?

"You good?" Jay asked with a concerned look on his face.

"My brother said my girl got shot." Those words didn't even sound right leaving my mouth. "I have to go see about her." I almost didn't recognize my own voice. I had never been a weak ass nigga, but the fear of Alex being dead damn near broke me all the way down.

Jay stood up. "Is she okay? Do you need me to drive you?"

"Nah, I'm good. I may be hitting you up soon though because something is telling me I might need a lawyer." I didn't know who, but somebody had to pay for this. I didn't even care if it was some accidental shit, a drive-by, or whatever. Whoever pulled the trigger of the gun that shot Alex would have to feel me if I ever found out who they were.

I didn't even feel like calling the hospital to see if she actually was there. I just got in my car and headed in that direction. My nerves were bad as shit, and for as anxious as I was to get to the hospital, I was damn near dreading it at the same time. If I got there and they told me something that I didn't want to hear, it would be all bad. It took me less than twenty minutes to get to the hospital. My phone was blowing up like crazy, but I ignored every call as I headed into the emergency room entrance. I saw Alex's mom in the waiting room with her girlfriend, and I headed towards them. Ms. Bianca had her head down, and she didn't look up until I was right up on her. Her face relaxed when she realized it was me.

"Hi, Panama." Her voice cracked. "I would have called you, but I don't have your number."

"That's okay. How is she?"

"I don't know yet. She got shot in the f-f—" Alex's mom started crying, and she couldn't even finish her sentence. Her girlfriend comforted her while looking at me.

"She got shot in the face, the arm, and the thigh."

My chest damn near caved in. A muhfucka shot my girl in the face? I couldn't even steady my breathing, I had to get up out of there. I turned around and headed for the exit with murder on my mind. Inside my car, I rolled a blunt and smoked it as if hospital security didn't patrol the grounds frequently, but I didn't care. All I kept thinking about was the fact that someone shot my shorty in the face. I allowed the weed smoke traveling through my body to relax me as much as it could, but my left leg was still bouncing up and down anxiously. This was some bullshit, but I swore to God on everything that I loved that if I ever found out who in the hell shot my girl, shit would be all bad for them and everybody that loved them.

# ALEX

*I* could tell that I was in bed. The heat had the room warm and toasty, and I heard the beeps of machines all around me. My throat was extremely dry. Pain radiated through my body, and I winced even before opening my eyes. I could feel a huge bandage, or something, taped to the side of my face. My eyelids felt heavy and I struggled to open them, but after a few flutters, I could see, but the bright light in the room caused me to squint. I was in a hospital room. The first person I saw was my mom and then her girlfriend Monica. As soon as I turned my head in their direction, my mom jumped up out of the chair that she'd been seated in.

"Baby, I'm so glad you're awake. Oh my god." She rushed over to the bed and kissed my forehead. "Are you in pain? Do you need me to call the nurse? Hold on, let me get somebody." My mom's words were flying out of her mouth so fast, she didn't even give me time to answer her questions before she ran off to find the nurse.

Monica gave me a comforting smile as I tried to figure out why I was in the hospital feeling like I'd been run over by a truck. "Do you remember what happened?" Monica asked just as images from that night began to flood my brain, and my heart started pounding in my chest hard and fast as hell. It was dark outside and hard for me to see, but I knew that figure. The mannerisms, the voice, it was one that I'd lived with for years.

Panama assured me that Quadim was dead, but he couldn't be. Tears spilled over my eyelids as I recalled Quashon on my phone sounding terrified. Had he played me? The little boy that I spent two years caring for and worrying about, did he really lure me to the house so Quadim could shoot me? *"If I can't have you bitch, nobody ever will."*

He stood over my body with that sadistic ass voice and said those words to me. My hand flew up to my face. I remembered him aiming the gun right at my face, and I turned my head and screamed as he shot me in the side of the face. Was I disfigured? My mom, the nurse and a doctor filed into the room as more tears rolled down my cheeks.

"Hello. My name is doctor Warren, and you ma'am are a very lucky young woman. You were shot three times, but each bullet went straight through, and you didn't have to have any surgery. Your vitals are good and as long as they remain that way, you can be released in about two days. You will of course be very sore, and you won't want to put any real pressure on your leg for a few weeks. You were shot in the jaw, so talking, eating, and chewing will be painful for a few weeks, but luckily you were shot with a small caliber gun. You will heal up just fine."

I didn't want to be vain, but I breathed a sigh of relief when he said I would heal up fine. Even though I'm sure Quadim was trying to kill me, I knew he'd love nothing more than for me to live and be disfigured so no one else would want me. I fought back tears as I thought about how I really stayed that long with a man that would rather take my life than to see me with someone else. That shit was absurd.

The doctor of course asked me if I knew who shot me, and I told him no. It wasn't even about me wanting to protect Quadim. I didn't care if he went to jail or hell. The thing is, Panama assured me that Quadim was dead, so maybe I was bugging that night and thought I saw him. I didn't know what in the world was going on. The nurse put some pain medication in my IV as I tried to tell the doctor that I didn't remember. He was right as fuck. Trying to talk hurt like hell, and I knew I wouldn't be doing much of it. My stomach rumbled, and it hit me that I was hungry, but how in the heck could I eat? The nurse heard my stomach and offered me a small smile.

"I'll give this medication just a few minutes to kick in. Once the pain has subsided, I'll bring you an Ensure. While you're not in any pain, it'll be easier to just drink that through a straw. I gave you the good stuff, so you should be able to drink it with little to no discomfort. Unfortunately, for probably the next four or five days, you'll have to be on a liquid diet. What kind of Ensure do you prefer?"

I just stared at her for a moment. The thought of opening my mouth was dreadful. My mom knew I was in pain and spoke up. "Chocolate? She doesn't like strawberry milkshakes or ice cream. Chocolate is her favorite."

I nodded my head, grateful for my mom. "Okay then, I'll be right back with it."

She for sure gave me the good stuff, and it didn't take it long to kick in at all. As the doctor and nurse were leaving the room, my heart smiled to see Panama coming in with flowers, a teddy bear, and about fifteen balloons. He looked crazy as hell walking with all those balloons behind him, but I loved him for it. He walked over to my bed with anger blazing in his eyes, but he still leaned down and kissed me on the lips. At times, I wished that we wouldn't have hooked right back up. I didn't want Panama getting in any trouble behind me. It would kill me if Quadim's bitch ass was the cause of him going back to prison. I couldn't wait to tell him who I thought it was that shot me, so he could get Castillo on it right away.

After I drank the Ensure, drowsiness took over, and I was unable to keep my eyes open. I guess I was out for a few hours because when I woke up, it was dark outside, and my mom and Monica were gone.

Panama was the only person in my room, and he was talking to Butta on the phone. I was still groggy, but I had to pee. The nurse told me to buzz her for a bed pan if I needed one, but I wanted to use the bathroom. I winced from the pain as I sat up.

"Butta let me call you back. What up shawty? Where you going?"

"To the bathroom," I grimaced.

"Hold up, let me carry you."

As soon as Panama stood up, I scooted to the edge of the bed and something very warm ran out of my vagina. I didn't have on underwear, and I could tell whatever was coming out of me was thick. I looked down in horror as blood saturated the sheets, and a huge blood clot the size of a golf ball oozed out of me and landed on the floor. Then, I passed out.

* * *

It had been an exhausting twenty-four hours. I still hadn't had a chance to tell Panama that I thought it was Quadim that shot me. Once I came to, the doctor did an ultrasound and confirmed that I'd miscarried and that I'd been around seven weeks. I had no clue that I was pregnant but ever since I left Quadim for real, I hadn't even been bothering with my birth control like that. I'd been so consumed with other shit, I foolishly assumed that maybe I wouldn't get pregnant quick because I'd been on birth control for five years. Because of the birth control, some months my period didn't even come. I hadn't been paying attention to any of that.

To say that Panama was pissed was an understatement. Someone had shot me and killed our child. It didn't take a genius to surmise that he had murder on his mind. Finally, the police were gone, and all of my visitors were gone. My father and Talisha were currently on a flight, and I knew that Panama and I wouldn't have much time alone. The nurse had just put pain medication in my IV, so my jaw had eased off enough so that I could try and talk. As soon as we were alone, I started talking.

"Panama, I think you made a mistake. I think it was Quadim that shot me. He's not dead."

A look of confusion covered his face. "What? What you mean he's not dead? Castillo beat the nigga half to death, and I finished him. I shot him."

"He shot me too. But I'm not dead." I grabbed my phone and sent him a text message detailing how Quashon had called me and what transpired from there.

Panama read over the message with a scowl on his face. When he was done, he looked up at me. "The lil' bastard that you were so concerned about, the lil' nigga that you lost sleep over, he set this up?"

I didn't say anything. I didn't know what to believe anymore, so I for sure wasn't going to make any effort to defend Quashon. Panama stood up. "I'm about to step outside and call Castillo. Normally when his team gets rid of bodies, they make sure the remains are never found again. I'm getting to the bottom of this shit ASAP. I'll be right back."

Panama left the room, and I stared up at the ceiling. I wanted solid food so bad the shit was ridiculous. I was tired of Ensure, Jell-O and chicken broth. If Quadim had in fact shot me, I wouldn't rest until Panama put him in the dirt. If I didn't put him in the dirt myself.

# NATALIA

"Where you going?" my mom asked me as she blew cigarette smoke from her nose.

"To see Alex," I grumbled with an attitude which my mother noticed right away.

"The fuck you mad about?" she snapped before taking a deep pull from her cigarette.

"Because Ma, I'm supposed to have a quiet background while I work. You all in here hollering for Candy, won't turn the TV down. I need to be working as much as I can, so I can get my own place, but I may have to take some time off until I can make other arrangements."

My mother snaked her neck and looked at me like I had two heads or something. "Well excuse the fuck out of me for living in my own damn house. You want me to tip toe around this muhfucka for eight hours while you work? If you cared about your job so much, you shouldn't have gotten kicked out of your house for lying to your nigga. Then you'd still be working in an environment suitable for you. I don't have to accommodate your needs little girl."

I snatched my car keys off the coffee table and stormed outside. I hated it at my mother's house. I damn near hated her. Tough love was the only love she knew. She acted like she never made mistakes or that she was perfect. You wanted to be coddled, comforted, or motivated, then don't talk to my damn mother. She's the most negative person alive. Tears streamed down my face and dripped off my chin as I got in my car and slammed the door. I knew better than anyone that I had fucked up. I'd been working eight hours a day for the past three days since Leonard put me out. I needed a nice paycheck or two so I could move, but my mom was going to mess that up. It was easy working from home when I lived with Leonard, but it would be impossible at my mom's house, and she wasn't even trying to be understanding.

Even though Alex and I weren't on good terms, I was still going to visit her because she was my cousin, and I loved her. Plus, if I had to stay at my mom's house for one more second, I would scream. I was reminded every second of every day of just how bad I'd messed up. I was sure that Leonard hated me, and he had every right to. The fact that Leonard, a man who had barely ever cussed at me or raised his voice at me, had put his hands on me, oh I messed up big time. I wanted to find the bitch that sent him that picture and spit all in her face. My entire life was ruined, but I really had no one to blame but myself.

Once I entered Alex's room, my breath caught in my throat as I saw her father and Talisha sitting in the room. I hadn't seen her father since the night we had sex. As soon as I walked in the room, my face flushed from embarrassment as I recalled our fuck fest in his backyard. "Hey Natalia," Talisha was the first one to speak, and she sounded all chipper. I was the scum of the Earth.

I smiled and prayed that it didn't look fake or forced. "Hi. Hey Ryan. Hi Alex. How are you feeling?"

She sighed as if she was exhausted. "I'm okay I guess. Just ready to go home tomorrow."

I sat down, and thankfully because Ryan and Talisha did a lot of the talking, I didn't have to say much. After about thirty minutes, I announced that I was going to the cafeteria. "Can you please bring me some type of soup or mashed potatoes? If I have to drink one more cup of broth, I'm going to scream."

"Sure." I left the room and headed for the elevators. I thought about the fact that Talisha was pregnant, and I wondered what would have happened if I had just left Leonard and told Ryan that I was pregnant by him. I'm sure it wouldn't have gone over well and in the end, even though it cost me my home and relationship, I knew that I made the right choice.

I was standing in the cafeteria contemplating on what I wanted to eat, when Ryan walked over to me. "What's up? Seeing as how you never came back to the house, we didn't really get a chance to speak after whatever happened, happened. I'm not even sure what to say now." He let out a nervous chuckle.

"There really is nothing to say. We were both very drunk, and it just happened. It's over. I will tell you though that I didn't come back to the house because Alex saw us, and she was pissed with me. She made me feel like shit, especially since Talisha welcomed me in with open arms."

Ryan's face fell, and I could tell he was shocked and embarrassed. "She saw us?"

I nodded. "Yeap. She may not have said anything to you, but she ripped me a new one. Add in the fact that I got pregnant, and shit went downhill from there. My boyfriend assumed it was his, but I knew it wasn't because he always pulls out. I snuck behind his back and got an abortion, and he kicked me out of the house. Ever since that one night in Miami, my life has been a shit show. I still don't even regret it though. Isn't that some shit?" I let out a light laugh while Ryan looked at me with his mouth hanging slightly open.

He ran a hand down his face. "You got pregnant?" he asked in a hushed whisper. "Yo this shit is crazy. Yeah, I was wildin' for real that night." Ryan shook his head. "I'm sorry you're going through all that. Where are you staying?"

I rolled my eyes. "With my mom for the moment, but hopefully I can be out of there in the next few weeks. I don't even care if I have to take out a loan or something."

"I feel bad as hell for real. Look, I put a lot of money into that smoothie bar, and now I'm saving for the baby with Talisha, so it might not be a lot, but just send me your cash app. I'll send you something."

I couldn't even front like I wasn't relieved. I would never have asked him for anything, but he offered, so I was going to take that shit. "Thank you." I gave him a small smile.

After I gave him my cash app information, I walked off and proceeded to get my food and the things that Alex wanted. As I was heading back to the elevator, my phone chimed, and I looked down at the notification. A smile slid across my face when I saw that Ryan had sent me $400. It wasn't a whole lot, but it would for sure help. Now, I just had to figure out how in the hell to get my life back on track.

"You sure you don't mind me being here?" I asked Alex after Panama let me in their apartment.

She was home from the hospital and relaxing on the couch. When I went to visit her, I was venting about my mom, and she told me I could come use her computer and internet since she'd be home for the next few weeks. I was so grateful. I didn't want to intrude on her, but it was the last week of the pay period, and I needed a nice check. I applied for a townhouse from a private owner, so he didn't really care about credit scores and all that. I maxed out a credit card to put the deposit down, but I didn't care. With my next check and the money that Ryan gave me, I was going to move into my apartment. I didn't care if I had to sleep on an air mattress.

"No, I don't mind. I'll just be watching television and in and out of sleep all day. It's fine. It's not like I can do much."

"Okay. Thank you so much." I was glad we'd gotten past our bullshit ass spat. Even though I had a sister, Alex and I were much more like sisters than cousins. We could get into it one day and be back cool the next.

As I logged into her computer and got everything that I needed set up, I watched discreetly as Panama brought her meds, food, drinks, etc., whatever she needed. He was being very attentive and sweet, but he was also thugged out with it. Lowkey how I wished Leonard was. I know it may sound stupid to want your man to be a thug. It's not like I wanted Leonard to sell drugs and shoot people, but I didn't even realize I was that attracted and turned on to gangsta ass niggas until I started fucking Ty Ty. I wanted a man to be sweet and loving with me, but I also wanted him to be rough and aggressive in the bedroom. I also liked a man whose presence alone commanded respect wherever he went. Leonard was just too soft and boring for me. I wasn't coveting my cousin's man, 'cus I would never, ever fuck behind her. I didn't want Panama, but I wanted a nigga like him for sure.

I had five minutes before I was supposed to clock in, and I sat there thinking about how I needed to get my life together. Lusting after thugs and whoever else wasn't going to fix my situation. I needed to be more focused on getting on my feet instead of fantasizing about the kind of man that I wanted. I clocked in and went about my work day. When I was done, I fixed Alex some soup, did a few things for her, and then I headed out to go to my mom's house. It was going on eight pm, so when I got in the house, I was just going to take a shower and go to bed. We weren't really on speaking terms, and I was just laying my head there. I couldn't wait to move into my own place. The Bible said I had to respect my mother. It didn't say that I had to deal with her. Once

I got into my own place, I would go back to feeding her with a very long-handled spoon.

"The fuck?" I grumbled to myself when I got outside and saw that a white Range Rover was blocking me in. I looked around, and there wasn't a driver in sight. I was ready to get something to eat and then go home and get in the bed. I jerked my car door open with an attitude as I wondered how long I would have to sit and wait for the inconsiderate ass person to move their vehicle.

I had only been in my car for about two minutes when a fine ass man walked up to my car. Baby was dressed in a red Polo sweater, a blue Polo bubble vest, dark denim jeans, and wheat-colored Timberlands. On his head was a red Polo toboggan. Dude stood about 6'1 with almond-colored skin and almond-shaped, light brown eyes. Being that he was dressed nice and warm, there wasn't a lot of his body that was visible to me, but I saw tattoos on his neck and his hands. His beard was trimmed up nice and neat, and no lie, my panties instantly became moist from my arousal. My annoyance melted away as I damn near salivated at the mouth over this man. It took me a second to realize that he was waiting for me to roll my window down. I was sitting there stuck on stupid, and I hoped he didn't notice. I rolled my window down, and he licked those succulent pink lips.

"My bad ma. I was just checking my mailbox. I didn't mean to block you in." He had a thick accent, and I could tell that he was from up north.

I forgot all about being pissed and offered him a small smile. I just couldn't find it in me to be rude to his handsome ass. "It's okay. I wasn't waiting long."

"You sure? I can't take you out to dinner to make it up to you? Wait, my bad, that was backwards as fuck. I'm supposed to ask if you're single first right?"

There was a gleam in his eye like a hungry lion that had spotted his prey, but I ignored all of that. "Yes, I am single."

"Word? I'm Jovaughn. You live out here?"

"No, my cousin does. My name is Natalia."

"Natalia, I like that. So I can take you to dinner?"

"Sure."

"Bet. Let me get your number." He pulled his phone from his pocket, and I observed that it was all there. That thugged out bad boy stance that I'd so desperately begun to crave lately. The potent smell of his cologne wafted through my window, and I had to have him.

I rattled off my number to him, and he promised to call. I ignored all the signs that he looked like trouble. Instead, from the moment I started my car to go home, my internal clock started ticking, and I was already waiting for his call.

# PANAMA

I stared at Diesel as blood poured from the gash on his forehead. Castillo had called a meeting in a warehouse. Present were me, Diesel, and ten other members of Castillo's team, be it mules, security, or niggas that sold dope for him. He walked in a circle around Diesel. It was strange as hell seeing a man as big and strong as Diesel bleeding and looking fearful of Castillo. A man that probably didn't weight 180 on a good day. Castillo stopped walking and looked out at all of us.

"When I tell a muhfucka to do something, I not only want it done, but I want it done the right way. How in the fuck did Quadim get up out of that ditch alive? Huh?" He stared back in Diesel's face.

"I-I thought he was dead Boss. He didn't have a pulse."

That statement caused Castillo to chuckle. "He didn't have a pulse. You got damn Doogie Howser MD nigga? You can pronounce people dead and shit? When have you ever known me to leave a body? That's what the fuck rivers and meat grinders are for. That's what the fuck my tiger is for, dumb ass nigga!" Castillo for real had a tiger in the back yard at one of his houses.

That's when I knew he was rich for real. Rich and crazy as hell. His backyard was big as hell, and the tiger was fenced in, in a huge enclosure. There's even a small ass pool for him to get in and cool off. Animal rights activists and shit didn't like it, but with the trees, pool, and all the space, he got plenty of exercise. Castillo told me it cost him $2,500 a week just to feed the damn tiger. That shit was crazy as hell to me, but there was no reasoning with a nigga like Castillo.

"Castillo, I'm sorry. It won't happen again." At that point, Diesel was pleading.

"I run a million-dollar a week operation, and you got me out here moving like a fuck nigga. The fact that Quadim isn't dead, the fact that he's now my enemy and he knows too much about me is unacceptable. You really gave this fool the potential to have the upper hand. Mistakes like that can't be tolerated or forgiven."

Faster than anyone could blink, Castillo raised his arm and squeezed the trigger of his gun, putting a bullet between Diesel's eyes. I stared at his body with no type of remorse. I mean, whether he died or not, Quadim was out there still, so I didn't necessarily feel like Castillo should have killed him, but he did. The anger that I had for Quadim shooting Alex and making her lose our baby ran too deep and was too fresh for me to feel bad that Diesel was dead. Castillo looked over at his remaining security.

"Clean this shit up and do it right this time. Everybody else is dismissed. Panama, let me holla at you," he stated before walking outside of the warehouse. I got up and followed him out to the Escalade, and I got in the back where he was sitting.

I didn't say anything. Castillo began to speak right away. "In my line of business, beefing over trivial things can lead to a lot of unwanted attention and a loss of money. Whatever you and Quadim had going on before was none of my concern, but when you started handling *my* business, *my* money, and *my* product, you became my business. When he shot at you and your brother, he violated. I've never had issues with my team moving in such a sloppy manner, and this shit has me furious. Rest assured as soon as I lay eyes on Quadim, he's as good as murdered."

"This shit is way too personal for me, so I hope I find him before you do. I appreciate it though. I wasn't trying to get involved in any beef myself. I just got out of prison; I don't need any unnecessary heat coming my way, but I just crossed paths with a fuck nigga, and I had to get at him. Aside from that though, I just want this money."

"As we all do. I'll be in touch. In the meantime, let me know if you need anything. I'm actually going to Panama in a few weeks on business. Your pops is one of the first people that I want to see."

I smiled at just the thought of his ass. "Yeah as soon as I get off these papers, I'm going to see him myself. It's been far too long. When you see him, tell him my ass is there as soon as I can be."

"No doubt."

I got out of Castillo's car and into my own. This shit with Quadim was out of order for real and not some shit that I wanted to be dealing with. All of the wild shit that I was doing before prison, I didn't have the desire to do anymore. Clubs were cool, but I didn't have to be in one every weekend. If I wasn't making money, there was no need for me to be out on the block. Chilling with the homies was cool but after being around hundreds of niggas for five years, I'd rather be in the crib cuddled up with my old lady. None of this beefing shit and street shit was what I had in mind when I came home. I just had to get at Quadim before his ass got at me, and it was as simple as that.

*** 

"Stop looking so sad, I brought you food," I told Alex a few days later. I decided to head inside around seven pm which was very early for me. She had finally gotten to the point where she could eat, and her leg was better, but she'd still been moping around the house. There was a slight disfigurement in her jaw where she'd been shot that looked kind of like a dimple. I thought it was kind of cute, but Alex hated it. Ever since the shooting, she'd been depressed.

"I'm tired of sitting in this apartment. The shit sucks." She pouted as she took the food that I handed her.

I sat down on the couch. "I can't leave the state ma, but why don't I send you somewhere? Maybe Cancun or Hawaii. Somewhere warm where you can just chill in a hotel room and relax for a few days. Get your mind right."

"I've been here by myself most days while you're out. The thought of being somewhere else alone doesn't appeal to me. I'll just wait until you can go somewhere with me."

"You know what I was thinking?" I looked at her. "While I'm on these papers, I just sell this weed and stack my money. When I'm off the papers, we just travel and work on another baby and just live life. I'm not going back to prison. I refuse. I just wanna be out here with you doing sucka ass shit."

I finally got a smile out of her. "Why does it have to be sucka ass shit? Why can't you just be doing fun things with the woman that you love?"

"Same shit," I joked, and she hit me playfully on the arm. I placed my container of food on the coffee table and pulled Alex into my arms. "On some real shit though. Even though I was mad at you, I didn't see us being back together when I came home. When we linked back up, shit just felt right though. I can't even front. Every day I think about what that baby would have looked like or if it was a boy or a girl. I just want you shawty. I don't want any of this other shit," I confessed truthfully. "Even if we not living in a fancy ass house, driving foreign ass cars, as long as we not struggling, I just need you bae."

Alex looked up at me with tears in her eyes. "Awww, why the fuck you being so mushy? You're making me cry." She laughed before kissing me on the lips.

"'Cus it's true. I feel like I didn't protect you enough when it came to—"

Alex cut me off. "Don't even start with that. It's cool Panama. You didn't ask for any of this shit with me and Quadim. As I kept saying, he was my mess to clean up, and I didn't do that. Me even running to Quashon trying to save his ass, all that was on me. It's not your fault. Once I'm all better, I'm going to look for another job, and I'm just going to work for us. I want us to build. I want the big house and the foreign cars and all your big headed babies. I want that for us."

The way she gazed into my eyes, I knew she meant that shit. As soon as I killed Quadim, all the street shit was dead. It was going to be just me and my lady.

# NATALIA

It had been four days since I met Jovaughn. We talked on the phone a few times and we texted. I told him about the fact that I was moving and why I was working out of Alex's apartment. He knew I got off at four, so he suggested once I was off, I meet him at his car and ride with him so we could get a bite to eat. I was down. Even though I worked from home, I made sure to dress extra cute that day in red jeans that were so damn tight I could barely breathe, a denim blouse, and nude Louboutin heels that Leonard bought me one year for Christmas. I was rocking my natural curls after twisting my hair the night before, and I had light make-up on my face. As soon as I arrived at Alex's that morning, she asked me who I was looking all cute for, so I told her about Jovaughn.

As always, she gave me her honest opinion and told me not to move too fast but other than that, she didn't seem too against it. When I walked out of her apartment, I saw Jovaughn walking towards his car. "You riding with me?" he called out across the parking lot.

I didn't mind riding with him and coming back to get my car once we were done. It was my last night in my mom's house, and the less time I had to spend there the better. I'd been working my ass off so I could have overtime hours, and my bank had given me a loan, so operation move into my own spot was underway. My mom and I were still barely speaking and after I moved, it would be a while before I went back to her house. I would do as I always had and love her from a distance.

"I can," I stated as I headed towards his vehicle. I couldn't deny the fact that Jovaughn was fine as fuck. I watched him as I got closer, and I noticed that he was bowlegged as hell, and that shit turned me on. It was kind of warm out for the time of year, and he was dressed in black True Religion sweats and a white, black, and red, long-sleeved True Religion shirt with black suede Timbs.

He popped the locks on the car, and I opened the door and climbed inside. "You look nice today." He glanced over at me as he popped a piece of Big Red gum into his mouth.

"Thank you. Where are we going?" I inquired as he started the car.

"I was thinking of taking you to Annette's Kitchen? Have you ever eaten there?"

"No, I haven't."

Jovaughn closed his eyes for dramatic effect. "Mannn, when I tell you that shit is like that. My aunt works there. Don't get it twisted, I still have to pay, but she blesses me and the food is so good. It's a lil' seafood spot. They have everything from snow crab legs, to alligator bites, and frog legs. I promise you their cheddar biscuits make Red Lobster's taste like shit."

I frowned my face up slightly. "I don't know about the alligator or the frog, but I love seafood, and I love a good cheddar biscuit, so it sounds good to me."

"You got everything under control as far as you moving tomorrow?"

The fact that he asked earned him a few cool points with me, but so far, I liked everything about Jovaughn. "Yes. I don't have anything big to move. When my ex and I broke up, he kept the house and all the furniture. All I have is clothes and shoes. I'm getting a television and a bedroom set delivered. My living room is going to have to stay empty for another month or so. I'm just ready to get my internet hooked up. Being able to work from home is going to be a blessing. My supervisor already approved me for all the extra hours I want, so my ass is going to be working six days a week, no less than ten hours a day." I was making $11 an hour, so that overtime was going to come in handy.

Jovaughn nodded his head. "I respect that. My sister works in a call center and no matter how much overtime they offer or how broke she is, she refuses to work overtime. I've seen her do that shit once, and that's when she wanted to go to Dubai with her friends. She lives at home and doesn't have any responsibilities. All of her money goes to clothes, shoes, partying, bundles, nails, and trips."

"I remember those days. If I was smart, I would have been saving money, but as soon as the money came in, I was spending it. My ex paid all the bills though, so there's no excuse for me to not have at least saved twenty dollars out of each check. Lesson learned though." So far, Jovaughn hadn't asked why me and Leonard broke up, and I for sure wasn't going to volunteer the information.

"I feel you. Sometimes we have to learn the hard way. When I was in the streets heavy making hella money, I was just running through that money doing dumb shit. I was spending way more than what I was saving and when I got jammed up, I couldn't even afford a decent lawyer. I could barely afford to make bond. That was a huge eye opener for me."

During our second conversation on the phone, Jovaughn told me that he worked with his uncle at his moving company. I wasn't sure what his work hours were, but for some reason, I got the feeling that he still lowkey hustled. We kept the conversation flowing and before long, we were pulling up at the restaurant that he'd told me about. The place was kind of small, and they only had a good twelve tables, but thank God they weren't all full. I trusted his word that the food was good. Most small restaurants did have good food.

I was famished, and it took the food a while to come out, but it was worth the wait. I got fried shrimp, fried calamari, coleslaw, and French fries. The biscuits were good as hell just like Jovaughn said, and I got so full that I could barely move.

"You good? Need anything else?" Jovaughn asked once we were back in the car. A toothpick rested in the corner of his mouth, and he reached over and gently squeezed my thigh as he spoke.

Even though it was technically our first date, I wasn't upset or offended that he was touching on me. A tiny surge of electricity actually shot through my body the moment he touched me. "No, I'm fine."

"A'ight."

As we rode back to the apartment complex, I wondered if I was really ready to have sex with him. Leonard, Ty Ty, and Ryan. I had three bodies already and it was only February. On one hand, I was one of those free-spirited people that didn't get overly sensitive about sexuality. As long as two grown, consenting adults did what they wanted, who was anyone to judge? Yes, cheating on Leonard with Ty Ty was wrong, and I dropped the ball by not using protection with Ryan. I was foul for sleeping with both of them, but I was no longer in a relationship. I was single and free so there was no way I was going to allow myself to overthink it and stop myself from sleeping with Jovaughn. Now was the time to take advantage of the fact that I could get some good thug dick without feeling guilty about it afterwards.

I often wondered how Leonard was doing and if he would move on anytime soon. He hadn't even tried to reach out to me, and I didn't blame him. We pulled up in front of Jovaughn's building, and he looked over at me. "You wanna come in for a minute?" There was a hungry look in his eyes, and I knew it wasn't because he wanted food.

"Sure."

I followed him into his apartment. He lived on the second floor. His floorplan was exactly like Alex's, and to my surprise, it was decorated very nicely. When I started dating Leonard, his home was nice but basic. The longer we were together, I added décor here and there, and once I moved in, I really spruced the place up. I wasn't sure who had decorated Jovaughn's crib, but the couch set, curtains, area rug, and décor all went together very nicely. I noticed there were no pictures on the wall, but that was cool for him. His color scheme was brown, burnt orange, and gold.

I jumped a little bit when Jovaughn invaded my personal space and started kissing me hungrily. He wasted no time getting straight to the point. He squeezed my ass for a bit and my jeans warmed his hands up enough that when he slipped his hands underneath my blouse and started massaging my breasts, his hands weren't cold, despite us having just come from outside.

"You smell good," he moaned in my ear before devouring my neck. My head rolled back in ecstasy as I concluded that he was going to be the kind of lover that I liked. I suckled his bottom lip, and he unbuttoned my jeans and yanked them down.

We were standing in the living room and there was an open space in the wall where you could see directly into the kitchen. A long marble top counter separated the kitchen from the living room and at that counter Jovaughn had two barstools so a person could sit there and eat. He lifted me up and sat me on one of the stools which had a high back on it. He took my shoes off then my jeans and my panties. Jovaughn then reached into his back pocket, retrieved a condom, opened it, and pulled his dick from his sweats. It wasn't huge, but I was sure that it would get the job done. Once the condom was on his erect dick, he walked over to me, unbuttoned my blouse and pulled my breasts from my bra. He kneaded one while sucking the other. I moaned softly as I rubbed the back of his head. He came up and once again found my lips. Jovaughn slid a finger into my pussy and started finger fucking me while our tongues did a sensual dance. I normally didn't even like fingers in my pussy because fingers carried germs. I hadn't even had a chance to tell him my likes and my dislikes, and I hoped his finger wouldn't throw my damn pH balance off and give me BV or some shit. I didn't have too much time to dwell on it because as he sucked my nipple and moved his finger in and out of me, I grew wetter and wetter until my honey was running out of my middle and down the crack of my ass.

Jovaughn pulled his saturated finger from my slit and placed it in my mouth. I'd never done that before, but his freak level turned me on, so I put his entire finger in my mouth and sucked the juices off as I looked him in the eyes. He stood up straight and pulled my ass to the edge of the chair. With my legs resting in the crook of his arms, he entered me and had me holding on for dear life in no time. I prayed the barstool was sturdy as I reached my hands up over my head and gripped the counter with my hands. Jovaughn looked down and watched as his dick slid in and out of my pussy.

"What you want to do with this dick?" he asked as he looked in my eyes.

"I wanna ride it," I managed to moan.

Jovaughn went over to the couch, and I didn't even take the time to wonder why we didn't go in the bedroom. Maybe he was just that anxious for the pussy. Juices trickled down my inner thighs as I sauntered over to the couch, straddled him, and slid down on his dick. He was no doubt a freak, so I knew I could be open with him about what I liked. "Choke me," I panted as I stared him dead in the eyes. I saw a flicker of excitement in them, and within seconds, his hand flew around my neck. He squeezed tight enough that I could still breathe, but he got the desired effect across, and I came almost instantly. "Fuckkkk Jovaughn," I could barely get the words out because his hand was still around my neck.

"Damn, you like that shit?" he breathed before leaning up to bite my nipple.

"Yes. Fuck yes. Bite me again," I begged. Jovaughn bit my neck and squeezed my nipple at the same time, and my clit began to thump like it had a heartbeat. "I'm about to fuckin' come," I growled like a damn animal. Jovaughn squeezed my ass, digging his nails into my cheeks and he bit my bottom lip. That was all she wrote, and the floodgates opened.

"Got damn." Jovaughn smiled. "This pussy good as fuck." We switched positions, and he bent me over the couch and fucked me from behind. He smacked my ass, pulled my hair, and stuck a finger in my asshole as he fucked me savagely from behind. I came a total of three times. By the time we were done, my legs were weak, but I still put my clothes on and prepared to leave his apartment.

"Damn, I'll definitely be hitting you up. Soon," Jovaughn stated as he walked me to the door.

"Do that." I smiled. Once I was outside and headed back to my car, the smile on my face grew wider. It seemed as though sex with other people besides Leonard just kept getting better and better.

\* \* \*

"Alex, follow this dude on Snap," I said shoving my phone in her face.

A light scowl covered her face. "Who am I following and why?" She took my phone and looked at the screen.

"When I saved Jovaughn's number in my contacts, he came up in my Snap suggestions, but I don't want to follow him. That will look weird. So you can follow him and tell me what he posts," I stated, dead serious. It had been two days since I had amazing sex with Jovaughn. We'd talked once and he texted me since then, but he hadn't yet mentioned us going out again or having sex again. I didn't want to look like the stalker type, so I wasn't going to dare send him a follow request.

"Don't start your shit Natalia. You and that man haven't even known each other that long. I guarantee you if you see some shit you don't want to see you gon' be wildin'. I don't even be requesting niggas like that."

I kissed my teeth. "Dang Alex, take one for the team. He doesn't even know who you are. He's not going to think you want him because you request him." I was all moved in at my new spot, but after ten hours of working, I decided to stop by Alex's and bring her food from Applebee's. She was tired of being in the house and still borderline depressed, but I wouldn't even front. I did mainly bring her food because I was hoping to run into Jovaughn, but when I pulled up, I didn't see his Range. I had been at Alex's for an hour, and we were done eating.

"There." She held up her phone showing me that she sent him a request.

"Thank you." I hit her with a big smile, all the while giving myself a mental pep talk. I promised that I wouldn't trip too bad no matter what I saw. She was right. We hadn't been talking that long, and Jovaughn was single. No matter how good his dick was I had to accept the fact that he had the right to do whatever he wanted to do.

Fifteen minutes later, her phone chimed, and she looked down at the screen. "He accepted, but bitch I'm not watching his snaps just yet. I don't care if he doesn't know who I am. That looks mad thirsty. At least wait a good twenty minutes."

I nodded my head. "Bet." We were curled up on the couch watching a movie. I was really ready to go home and curl up in my bed, but I wanted to see if Jovaughn had any interesting snaps. My mama always said don't go looking for stuff if you're not ready for what you might find, but fuck it. I was going to go home, light some candles, drink some wine, and take a hot shower. I would love it if Jovaughn came over, but I wasn't going to ask him.

I needed money, but the customers that I dealt with daily were working my nerves. For the next few days, instead of doing ten hours, I would just do eight. I deserved a small break, but I loved being in my own place so much that I still wasn't taking any days off in the near future. I had ten hours of paid vacation time that I was saving for warm weather. I liked getting my own place and doing it mostly on my own, but I'd be lying if I said I didn't miss the days of Leonard paying for everything. Jovaughn for sure didn't look broke, and I lowkey hoped that in addition to breaking me off with good dick, he'd give me some money too.

Finally, twenty minutes had passed and as soon as I looked at Alex, she passed me the phone. My fingers were damn near trembling as I went to his name and pressed play on a snap from twenty-two hours before. Two more hours and it would have been gone, so I caught it just in time. I smiled as the video began to play. It was his sexy ass sitting in his car smoking a blunt and rapping along to a Nipsey Hussle song. Damn he was fine. The smile was quickly erased from my face though. The next snap was of him on a bed, but I couldn't exactly say he was lying on it since his head was resting on some bitch's ass. He was looking at himself in the camera, and then he started talking to her, asking her what she said.

"I said get yo' big head off my ass." The female only had on some white Marc Jacob boxer briefs, and her ass was big as shit.

My heart started pounding in my chest as Jovaughn sat up, smacked her on the ass, then put the camera in her face and started kissing on her neck. "Mooveee, stoppppp," she whined in an irritating ass voice trying to push him off of her.

He didn't keep the camera on her face for long, but I saw enough. She was light-skinned and had grey eyes. Her eyes made her ass look like the Incredible Hulk. No lie, shorty had a strong ass face. She wasn't cute at all to me. How you ugly with them pretty ass eyes? "Give me a kiss," he demanded, and made my heart skip a beat in the process.

That nigga told me he was single. If he wasn't single, she had to be very special for him to be flaunting her like that on his social media. The nigga slept with me two days before and was begging her manly looking ass for kisses. The messed up thing about it was I couldn't even say shit to him because then he'd know I'd been spying on him.

"He with a girl?" Alex asked curiously.

All I could do was nod my head. I was borderline embarrassed. My heart sank as the next snap played. I couldn't see because the room was dark, but a freaky ass Trey Songz hit played in the background. This nigga. I handed Alex her phone back. I tried so hard to front and hide my true colors because I didn't want to look pathetic. I should have left well enough alone.

"He's just the average nigga Natalia. Don't even trip. They probably have history."

"You're right. It's cool. I'm about to go home and take a bath though. I'll check on you tomorrow to make sure you're good."

"Okay. Thank you."

I let myself out and rushed out to my car. It was cold and unlike when I initially arrived, I didn't want to see Jovaughn. Lying ass bastard. Maybe she wasn't his girlfriend, but like Alex said, I believe they had some kind of history. He looked like he really loved her. How in the hell could I compete with that? I drove home feeling sorry for myself. As soon as I got inside I poured myself a glass of wine. I took three large gulps and headed towards the bathroom to turn the shower on. I drained the glass as I waited for the water to get good and hot. I wanted it damn near scalding. The wine went straight to my head and put me in my feelings. If I had just been faithful and stayed with Leonard, I wouldn't be going through any of this. But which was better? Being loved, adored, and cherished by a man that I wasn't happy with, or getting bomb ass dick from a thugged out dog?

I stripped out of my clothes and walked in the kitchen naked to pour myself another glass of wine. Damn, I was no Lauren London, but I looked way better than that muscular broad that Jovaughn was hugged all up on. She wasn't really muscular, but her facial features were too damn strong for her to be a woman. Shorty didn't have shit on me when it came to looks so Jovaughn had to love her ugly ass. I sipped from my glass as I walked back towards the bathroom. Oh well, it was what it was. I didn't need to be jumping into a relationship anyway. Jovaughn had some bomb ass dick but if I didn't get it again, I would have to live with the memories.

I was drinking the wine fast, so it went right to my head so much so that as I lathered my body with soap, I let out a light giggle. I couldn't believe that I was in my own place alone. I felt bipolar as hell because one minute I welcomed the change and the next, I was thinking of Leonard and how life would be if I didn't have a lowkey fascination with thugs. I spent a good ten minutes in the shower, and then the heat from the water ran my ass up out of there. Hot water and wine didn't really mix. There was a thin coat of sweat covering my upper lip. After I wrapped my towel around my body, I was shocked to see that Jovaughn had called my phone.

I held the phone in my hand and stared at it as I contemplated whether or not I wanted to call him back. The wine coursing through my body made me forget all about being angry with him. Before I could figure out if I wanted to return the call, he texted me and asked if I felt like company. That time, I didn't hesitate to reply with a simple yes. Fuck the Incredible Hulk. I wanted some dick.

## QUADIM

"*D*amn," I mumbled at the girl's huge ass that was standing in front of me in the gas station. Shorty was bad as fuck. Her ass was big, hips wide, and thighs thick. I knew she heard me because she turned around with a scowl on her face, but I simply raised my eyebrow at her.

I'm sure she got unwanted attention all of the time, but if she didn't like the shit, she should dress different. The jeans she had on looked painted on, so you damn right I was going to look. What nigga wouldn't? She smirked and turned around to pay for her stuff. I don't know why the sudden urge hit me, 'cus I really don't be tricking on females like that, but something came over me. I walked up behind her and placed my juice on the counter with her stuff. "Let me get a pack of Backwoods, and I'm paying for this shit too."

Shorty turned around again but that time, she had a seductive look on her face. She looked me up and down as she bit her bottom lip. Yeah, I thought she'd change that tune quick. Shorty turned back around and passed the cashier a hundred-dollar bill. "Nah, I'll pay for mine and his too."

I had to stop my mouth from falling open in shock. She got my ass good. After the cashier handed lil' mama her change, and she turned to leave the store, that's when I saw the sides of her bodysuit were cut out and she didn't have on a bra. Her breasts were small, but they sat up nice and pretty. My damn dick was harder than steel sizing shorty up. "Damn, wait up," I called after her and attempted to catch up.

Since being shot in the head, sometimes my coordination seemed off. A lot of shit about my body felt different. Some days, I would be about to do something and then forget what it was. I would literally have to rack my brain for a minute to remember what it was. I hated that shit, and it just reminded me that I wanted Panama and Castillo dead. I'd checked the news and the obituaries, and there was no mention of Alex, so I could only assume that her ass was still alive. After I killed Panama, she'd wish she was dead.

Ole girl stopped walking and turned around to face me. "Let me guess, you want my number?" She was brown-skinned and had on a curly, red lacefront wig. She was cocky as fuck, borderline arrogant, but the way her thighs were damn near bursting out of her jeans, I let it slide. Truth be told, I still loved Alex, but we could never be. Not after she violated the way she did; plus, I did try to kill her. Lynn was cool, but she'd been acting all shaky and weird since I shot Alex. Some days, she was distant, but I didn't give a fuck. It just let me know that she wasn't built for a nigga like me. I needed a thorough shorty on my team. One that understood that the penalty for betrayal was death.

"Something like that." I smirked as I fantasized about fucking her into submission.

"You didn't even ask me if I was single."

"Shorty it's cold as fuck out here. I know you have to be cold." I glanced at her side boob. "Let's cut the games and the small talk. You trying to give me your number and your name or what?"

For a second, she looked like she wanted to curse me out. Finally, she did as I requested and cut the bullshit. "The name is Robin. You are?"

"Quadim." She gave me her number, and I headed for my car. Despite the fact that I was looking forward to climbing in between her thighs, I still had a lot to be pissed about. Being shot cost me a month's worth of money because I was laid up trying to heal, and I couldn't make money like that. Once I got well enough to come home, I put Quashon out there moving my product, but that still wasn't the answer that I needed. Because he spent most of the day in school, he couldn't hustle until school was over, which meant I was still missing money.

I was hopefully about to handle Castillo though. I knew enough about his operation to tip the FEDS off to a few places where he did business. I gave them addresses and specific details. I knew that Castillo had police on his payroll, so I didn't bother to call bullshit Crime Stoppers at our local police station. For all I knew, he had some FEDS on his payroll too, but it was easier for me to get him locked up than for me to kill him since he always had security with him. Even if I lucked up and was able to pump a few bullets into him, one of his men would murder me before I could flee the scene.

It had been four days since I had ratted him out, and I was anxious to know if that shit would work. I needed him off the streets by the time I got ready to show my face and do business again. Quashon moving the work would do for a moment, but I had to get back to it. Just in case Castillo did have some FEDS on his payroll, I was as careful as I could be. I called from a simple ass cell phone out of Wal-Mart. It wasn't a smart phone and cost about forty bucks. I didn't even go in and get it; I got a fiend to go in and get it for me. On top of that, I disguised my voice. There was no way the shit could come back on me. Once Castillo was off the streets, the only person I would have to worry about was Panama.

I was tired, so I headed home. I would wait a few days before I called Robin because her lil' conceited ass was probably thinking that I'd call her right away. I needed to get my body back right before I tried to knock the lining out of her pussy. Pain pills gave me stamina when I had sex. I found that out when I fucked Lynn a few days ago, but I paid for that shit afterwards. I should have just laid there and let her do all of the work. When I got home, I didn't see Lynn's car, and I was hoping that she wouldn't come through. At one point, I did hope me and Alex could work shit out, but even when I discovered that we couldn't, I still didn't want to hop into anything with anyone else. I wanted to enjoy being single. At first, I just wanted Lynn to help me with Quashon, but fuck that. He was turning sixteen in a few days. It was time for me to stop treating him like a baby.

As I pulled up in the driveway, I saw him walking up the sidewalk. I hadn't seen the lil' nigga smile since Alex left. He never looked happy. No matter what he was doing whether it was playing the game, eating, or watching TV, he always had a slight frown on his face. It bothered me a lil' bit. I didn't ask for the responsibility of raising him, but he was my brother, and I wanted him to be happy.

"What's good? You hungry? Order a pizza," I stated after we got in the house.

"Okay," he mumbled as he pulled my money from his pocket. As soon as he got out of school every day, he hit the block for me. I counted the money then looked over at him.

"I'm taking you to get your license on your birthday. You can have Alex's Benz."

Quashon's eyes and face lit up in a way that I'd never seen him light up before, and it made me feel good. "Word? For real Quadim?"

"Word. I don't drive it. It's just sitting there, and it's too cold for you to be walking. You 'bout to be sixteen, you need a car."

"Thanks," he beamed as he pulled out his phone to order the pizza. It was the least I could do for him. He was already doing things that a grown man did, so he may as well have a car.

# ALEX

"You good?" Panama asked as I came out of the bathroom. It was my first time not using my crutch since being released from the hospital. I was even about to take it a step further and go to Target. If I had to sit in the house one more day, I would scream. I could also finally use my arm and go a whole day without taking any pain medication.

"Yeah I'm good." I walked over to the mirror to attempt to do something to my hair. I'd been wearing it up in a bun since I got shot. I just wanted to go shopping, get a few new things, wax, mani, pedi, all that shit. I wanted to feel like a new woman. My pussy was wolfing, eyebrows needed to be arched, shit was bad, but Panama was right there every day by my side like I was perfect. I knew he was mad that we lost the baby. I was upset too, but there wasn't anything that we could do about it. All of my time sitting on the couch hadn't been in vain though. I'd enrolled in school. I wanted to become an LPN and eventually an RN.

I'd also been experimenting and testing a lot of natural recipes for skin care items. I made a facial cleaner that smelled good as fuck and left my skin soft as hell and the two main ingredients were honey and lemon juice. Panama wrapped his arms around my waist and placed his face in the crook of my neck. His body was pressed into mine, and I could feel that his dick was hard.

"You feel good enough to give me some?" he asked in a hopeful voice before placing a soft kiss on my neck that sent a shiver down my spine.

I chuckled. "Panama. I haven't been waxed in almost two months. That bush is mean."

"Mannn, if you think that's 'bout to stop me you crazy as hell. If you're in pain or you don't feel like it, that's one thing, but some hair on ya pussy. Nah nigga, come with a better excuse than that."

I turned around to face him. I was kind of horny myself. "Don't say I didn't warn you. If something reaches out and grabs you, it's your fault."

He erupted into laughter. "You wild as fuck shawty. But nah, for real though. When we gon' try for another baby?" He turned serious as he stared into my eyes and waited for an answer.

"I start school in three weeks, so I won't be ready for at least another year. Is that okay?" I knew what I wanted mattered, of course, but I cared about how Panama felt too.

"Yeah baby, we can wait a year. That'll give me time to stack some paper. I'll never try to get in the way of you chasing a bag. We gon' be something like a power couple huh?"

I nodded as my lips found his and our tongues did a sensual dance. We rocked back and forth slowly as we kissed. "Damn I been missing this pussy," he mumbled into my mouth as he pulled my leggings and my panties down. I broke the kiss so I could pull my PINK hoodie over my head.

Panama and I ended up on the bed, where he placed kisses from my ankle all the way up to the inside of my thigh. I was self-conscious since my pussy had an afro, but he acted as if it didn't bother him.

From my belly to my breasts, then my cheek where I'd been shot, Panama placed soft, sensual kisses on my flesh, and tears burned my eyes. I was blessed to be alive, and I was blessed to have him in my life. I'd been given second chances twice. It didn't get better than that. Panama moaned as he eased his dick inside me.

"You crying?" he asked, looking alarmed.

I had to chuckle. He looked confused as hell. "I'm just emotional because I'm blessed, and I love you."

Panama moved slowly in and out of me. "I love you too shawty. Always and forever." I wrapped my legs around his waist, and Panama sexed two orgasms out of me before he came. I knew he came quick because we hadn't had sex in a lil' bit.

"Do I need to come to Target with you?" he asked once I was dressed again. "Castillo has eyes looking for Quadim, but he hasn't had any luck yet. Quashon hasn't been in school in the past few days either. He'll be the best lead to Quadim."

Knowing Quashon, he was probably suspended. Quadim really needed to get his act together for his brother, but I doubted he ever would, and at this point it didn't really matter. Quadim was a dead man walking. It bothered me that Quashon's birthday had just passed, and I couldn't even call him and wish him a happy birthday. I wasn't sure if he had set me up to be shot and because of that, I'd never deal with him again. I knew Castillo was a ruthless man, and I hoped that he wouldn't kill Quashon along with Quadim. Even if I was unsure about him, I didn't want the child dead. Quadim just had him living too fast, but I couldn't tell him anything about Quashon. That was his brother, his life, his family.

"No, I'm fine." I was too excited about leaving the house to be nervous. I just wanted my life to become normal. I finally had a boyfriend that wasn't a sadistic piece of shit. Now, I just wanted to be able to roam freely without fear of getting shot or attacked by a psycho. The more I thought about it, I wasn't bugging that night. Yeah, it was dark, but who else had a reason to shoot me? They didn't rob me or car jack me, just shot me and left me for dead. It had to be Quadim. The fact that he was still alive and lurking made me shudder, but he'd get what was coming to him soon enough.

"You sure?"

I kissed Panama on the lips. "Yes, I'm sure. I have a lot of shit to do, and I don't want to hold you up. I'll be aight." I pulled my .22 from my purse to show Panama that I was strapped, and a look of relief crossed his face.

"Bet. Call me if you need me."

I left the apartment and thought about how my life was about to change for the better. I was excited about making more skincare products to sell. I had to play around with a few more ingredients before I perfected the cleanser and the moisturizer. I didn't play about my skin so I'm always looking up natural products to use. I wanted to get some cute little packaging and make a website. I knew that it would take money to start, and I was prepared to invest all of my savings into it. I needed it to take off because it would be hard to work while I was in school, but I didn't want Panama taking care of all the bills. He always refused my help, but I still wanted to have money coming in because his selling drugs was only supposed to be part-time.

I used to sit in the house and think about how lucky Natalia was. I vowed that Quadim would be my last street nigga. I was ready to give a square guy a try, and she was running away from hers. Panama was a street nigga for sure, but that's not all he was. He had dreams and aspirations and more importantly, he had good sense. He loved me and treated me the way that I deserved to be treated, so I wasn't just going hard for myself. I was going hard for us, because as much as I deserved a good man, he deserved a good woman.

My phone rang as I was pulling into Target, and I saw that Talisha was calling me. "Hey," I answered the phone in a chipper voice.

"I guess I look like a whole gotdamn fool huh? Yo' bitch ass daddy really tried me and you, I thought we were cool Alex," Talisha yelled. I had a good idea of what she was talking about, but I needed to hear her say it.

"What are you talking about?" I barked in a defensive voice. Even though if she knew about my dad and Natalia, she had a right to be mad, she wasn't about to be coming at me foul.

"I let yo' hoe ass friend stay in my house, and she fucked my nigga! I knew it was strange that after the first night, she chose to go stay in a hotel instead of our house when we have all this extra space, but I decided not to dwell on it. I was looking in your dad's phone and saw that he sent her a cash app for $400 and I wanted to know what it was for. He tried real hard to play me like I was stupid, saying her dude put her out and she just needed help. After two days, I got the shit out of him. All y'all are foul. I'm pregnant going through this shit." She erupted into tears.

I took a deep breath and attempted to calm myself down. Talisha was only older than me by about ten years so I for sure didn't look at her as a stepmother type figure. Up until that moment, she'd always been cool. I knew she was pregnant and hormonal, but she'd better be mad with the right ones. "Okay first off, you need to watch how the fuck you're talking to me. I'm not the pussy police, and I for sure can't control what my dad does with his dick. I was talking to my man on the phone when those two did what they did and when I found out, I cussed Natalia out. I told her she was foul as fuck for doing what she did after you invited her into your house, and *she* decided then that she would stay at a hotel. I could be mad as I wanted to be at her but at the end of the day, what I look like telling you some shit? That's still my dad. I stay out of shit that's not my business."

"Me and you are supposed to be cool though Alex."

"And that's my dad! I get that you're upset, but if yo' damn sister or cousin or best friend fucked yo' nigga, would you tell me?" I screeched into the phone only to be met with silence. "Exactly! Don't call my phone with the bullshit. You never gave me a reason to disrespect you but bitch, I'm a grown woman just like you." I furiously tapped the end button to disconnect the call. She had me fucked up. I checked Natalia about what she did and that's all that I could do. I had been having a pretty good day until she called and ruined the shit. I was only concerned about my life, and I wanted everyone else to leave me out of their bullshit.

# QUASHON

"*B*out time you came back to school nigga. Where you been?" my best friend Trey asked me when I entered homeroom.

"Getting money." I slid into my desk as all eyes were on me.

I really didn't like school, but before I got the car, I really didn't like being outside in the cold hustling for Quadim either, so I would come to school and use it as an excuse not to hustle for him. Now that I had a car, I didn't have to stand outside, so I had better places to be than school. I only came after my birthday to stunt in all the shit Quadim got me, plus to show off my car. I was fresh as hell in a brand new True Religion outfit that cost Quadim over $300. I had on some fresh new J's, a gold chain with a diamond encrusted Jesus piece on it, and my draws were even new. I had on Polo boxers and Polo socks. My shoulder-length dreads were freshly twisted, and I felt like the man. I was the envy of the school. A sophomore pulled up in a Benz. Man, niggas' mouths hit the floor when I hopped out of that car. I already had a gun from when I was hustling. Quadim told me I better not let anybody rob me and take his work or he was gon' beat my ass. I'd rather kill a nigga than to have to go up against Quadim. When that nigga was angry, I'd seen him snap. Plenty of times, I was scared that he was gon' kill Alex. She was tough though, she always fought back. Until last time when he shot her. Quadim was my blood and I loved him, but a part of me hated him for shooting Alex. She treated me better than my own mother ever did, and Quadim was foul for that.

Still, there was only so much I could do. I mean, I'm a kid, and he's my brother. The only family that I really had. I wasn't trying to go to foster care, so I just did what he said. When I turn eighteen, I hope I could dip and get my own spot though. I grew up in the hood around gangs, so that shit wasn't foreign to me, but my closest friends had mothers that cared about them and some had fathers too. Quadim let me do whatever; I didn't even have rules at home to follow. My friends thought that was cool, but I didn't. Even when they got mad thinking their parents were tripping, I knew their parents were only trying to look out for them. Quadim didn't direct me away from the streets, he pushed me towards them. Sometimes, I wondered if he'd even care if I got killed. I liked how Alex used to be attentive and gave me talks and told me to do good in school. It made me feel like somebody cared about me for real.

"Nigga you fresh as hell. I wish I had somebody to put me on." Trey shook his head. "My moms was bitchin' this morning 'cus I asked her ass for five dollars. She work twelve hours a damn day and act like she don't want to give me five dollars."

I reached into my pocket and pulled out a five. "Here nigga." Truth be told, Trey didn't know how lucky he was. I was scared to get robbed, I was scared of getting shot, but that's not anything that I could tell Quadim. He'd probably beat my ass and call me a pussy. In the past few weeks, I made him more than $5,000 selling his drugs, and all he gave me out of it was $1,000. I was heated at first, but the car made up for it. I was slowly getting used to the role that he'd thrown me in. It was probably going to be my future anyway. He just sped the process up.

Trey's eyes widened with appreciation. "Good looking my nigga. What you doing after school? You trying to come by and play the game? Don't bring your car though. You know my mom is going to have a fit. She already side eyes you because of your brother."

I started to tell him fuck his mom, but I didn't. I also wanted to say fuck hustling and go do shit kids my age did, but I had to make Quadim's money. "I'll let you know," I grumbled as the bell rang signaling the start of first period.

I grabbed my bookbag and headed out of the classroom behind everyone else. "Quashon!" an annoying ass voice rang out.

I sucked my teeth and turned around, already knowing who it was. Just like I thought, when I turned in the direction of the voice, aggravating ass Natasha was coming towards me. Her big 5'8 ass got on my nerves. "What?" I didn't even try to hide the fact that I was annoyed.

She waltzed up to me with a scowl on her face. "What?" She snaked her neck. "I think it's fucked up how you got a baby by my cousin and you doing her real dirty. The baby was born on yo' hoe ass birthday, and you haven't even asked about him. You pulling up in a Benz like you the shit. Nigga you a dead beat!" she barked in my face.

I backed up with a frown on my face. "First of all, you better get out my face fo' I beat yo' ass. How I know that's my baby, 'cus she say so?" I didn't add in the fact that while Ebony had taken my virginity, she was far from a virgin when we fucked. She was seventeen and a sophomore. Shorty had way more experience than me. Her baby could have been mine, or she could have tried to pin it on me because she knew Quadim had money. I was honestly scared that it was mine. What in the hell could I do with a child? I barely remembered my mother, and I never knew my father. My grandmother was mean as shit, and Quadim didn't like kids.

"Yes! If you didn't trust her, you should have never been fucking her raw. My cousin isn't no hoe! How you're doing her is dirty. She should get her brother to beat your ass."

I sucked my teeth. "Girl fuck you, Ebony, and her brother. How about that?" I walked off and headed for my class in an effort to beat the tardy bell. I made it just in time and sat down in my seat.

I didn't want to be a deadbeat. I hated my mother and my father, and if Ebony's child was mine, I didn't want to be hated. I was only sixteen though. What was I supposed to do with a baby? Ebony lived in the projects in Durham sometimes. She stayed with her aunt in Raleigh too so she wouldn't have to switch schools when her mom got another job and moved. Her aunt worked a lot and when she wasn't working, she spent a lot of time with her boyfriend. Her two daughters lived with her, but they never said shit the times that Ebony snuck me in. A few times when Alex and Quadim weren't home, I snuck Ebony in my house. It wasn't even really sneaking because Quadim didn't care what I did. Alex would have probably said something, so to keep the confusion down, I just waited until she was gone. Ebony and I messed around for about five months before I found out her ex was still calling her. By that time, she was spending more time in Durham, and it was easy for me to cut her off. I started talking to other chicks and forgot about her, until one day she hit me up talking about she was two months pregnant. I was scared and didn't know how to react, so I told her to tell her ex and hung up on her. She was telling people it was my kid, but she never said anything else to me, so I figured maybe it wasn't mine. I saw a few pictures she posted on IG when she started showing, and I couldn't front, Ebony was fine as fuck. All the older dope boys wanted her, but she fucked with me.

I wanted to reach out to her, but I didn't know what to say. I had a car and a little bit of money, so I could visit her and give her money if the baby was mine. I didn't want to be taking care of another man's kid though. Thoughts of her and the baby plagued me all the way until the bell rang. I pulled out my phone and texted her and asked if I could see the baby. It took her two hours to reply to me and tell me that I could come by.

* * *

"What's up?" I asked as Ebony answered the door with a scowl on her face. She had a baby cradled in her arms, but I couldn't see his face because it was hidden by a fluffy blue blanket. Ebony had on short shorts and a tank top, and her once small breasts were big as shit. Her stomach had a pudge, and her thighs had gotten thicker. Her hair was pulled up on top of her head in a bun, and she looked tired. I knew I should have been out making Quadim's money, but it would just have to wait for a little while. I needed to go ahead and handle this baby situation.

She rolled her eyes and walked towards the couch. "You want to see him, here, but you don't have to say shit to me. I know you think he's not yours, and I'm not gonna beg you to take care of him. You haven't done shit for me thus far, and he still has everything he needs." She was pissed, but I guess maybe she had a right to be.

I walked over and held out my arms for the baby. I'd never in my life held a baby, and I didn't know what I was doing. "Watch his head," she instructed.

I sat down on the couch and stared into his little round face. He was light as hell like Ebony. My skin is the color of toasted almonds. I couldn't tell who the baby looked like, but he was cute for sure. He had a mass of jet black curls on his head, and he slept peacefully as I stared at him. I didn't know shit about being anybody's dad, but I could try.

"Look, I just knew that you started back talking to Isaac, so when you told me you were pregnant, I assumed it was his."

"Well maybe you shouldn't assume," she snapped. "He started back calling me, but I wasn't trying to fuck with him after he cheated on me with a dirty butt way before I started talking to you. He was begging, that's it. You just jumped the gun and got mad. You didn't even try to hear me out. I haven't slept with anyone since you. I'm not a hoe, despite what you may think." She crossed her arms over her chest. "I had to deal with my mom being pissed the entire time that I was pregnant. She wouldn't buy shit for the baby. I got all his stuff from my aunts, cousins, and hand me downs from my friend that had a baby last year. I don't have anyone to watch him so I can get a job, and I still have to go to school and maintain my grades so I can graduate next year. I don't know how I'm going to do it all, but I am," she stated with tears in her eyes making me feel bad.

"Look, I'm sorry aight?" I reached in my pocket and pulled out all the money that I had. "It's not much but it should be about three hundred dollars."

Ebony looked down at the money. I could tell she wanted to take it, but she was being stubborn. "It's not all about money either. I have homework to do and as soon as I put him down, he's gonna cry. You got an hour to watch him for me or you got better shit to do?" she asked with an attitude.

"Man, I'll watch him, do what you gotta do. Yo, what's his name?"

"Tristan. Thank you." Ebony took the money and stood up. She went towards the back of the house and came back with her book bag. I sat back on the couch and the baby started wiggling a little bit, but he didn't wake up. He smelled good as hell, and I inhaled his scent on the low. I peeked over at Ebony doing her homework, and I knew I had to be better than my parents and even Quadim. I really didn't want to sell drugs, but it seemed like at the moment that was my only option. I couldn't let Ebony do everything by herself. That shit wasn't right.

# NATALIA

I stared at Jovaughn as he ate his lobster, and I contemplated whether or not I should call him out on his shit. It had been a week since I saw his first snap, and last night, he had the Incredible Hulk on his snap again. That time, they were in Wal-Mart, and he was following her down the aisles rubbing on her butt and acting all touchy feely. He hit me up the next day asking if I wanted to go grab something to eat. In the week since I first saw her on his snap, we had sex two times. It got better each and every time. I was trying not to get dickmatized, but it was hard. He obviously had some shit with him, and I wanted to call him on it.

"Why you looking at me like that?" he inquired as he wiped his mouth with a napkin.

"I saw you last night at Wal-Mart with a girl. I know you're not my man. You're single, and you can do what you want, but I just need to know if you have a girl. I'm not into being a side chick," I stated in a non-confrontational manner. I hoped he didn't quiz me and ask me no shit like what Wal-Mart 'cus then I'd be fucked. Between Raleigh, Knightdale, Cary, and surrounding areas, there were a hundred Wal-

Marts. I just didn't want him to look at me like a creep for using Alex's snap to spy on him.

"I don't have a girl, but that's my ex. We got a crazy bond," he stated without batting an eyelash. He then shrugged a shoulder. "I mean, I am single. I spent six years with shorty though. We've been broken up for almost a year, but if she was to take me back, I can't front like I won't go."

That wasn't exactly what I wanted to hear, but I respected the fact that he was being honest. It seemed pointless to try and get to know him when he was basically just waiting on her to take him back, but I didn't really want to leave him alone. "What makes your bond so crazy?" I asked.

"The years man. We just have a lot of history. When I met her, she had a two-year-old son. She's not from here. All her family is in Baltimore including her baby daddy. She only has a cousin and a best friend here. I'm the only father figure that her son has ever known. She's a good girl. Held me down, always kept it a hundred, but I cheated on her quite a bit." He said it like it was no big deal. "She got tired of it and left my ass alone. I can't blame her, but I'm still there for her and her son. She's in school, and she doesn't work, so I help her out here and there."

Baggage with a capital B. If I was smart, I'd grab my shit, leave and never look back, but those succulent lips, the smell of his cologne, the redness in his eyes from the weed he'd smoked, his dope boy swag, it all made my pussy thump. I picked up the last jumbo shrimp that was on my plate, popped it into my mouth and chewed thoughtfully. Finally, I looked over at him as I wiped my hands on a napkin. "Why did you cheat on her?" I knew there could be plenty of reasons. Shit, I was a cheater myself. Leonard was a good guy just like he said Incredible Hulk was a good girl, and yet we both cheated. I for sure couldn't judge him when I had done my own dirt and plenty of it.

"Man you know that shit comes with the territory. Females are trained to latch onto niggas with money. A man with enough paper, any kind of looks and anything going for himself damn near doesn't even have to work for the pussy anymore. It gets thrown at us with both hands every single day. I don't know too many men that can resist the temptation, especially when some of the females are bad as fuck. I mean, supermodel type broads. The kind of females that you would think didn't even have to be thirsty. They'll offer you the pussy on a silver platter while telling you all the shit they wanna do to the dick. Who can turn that down every time? Not my ass. That's why for as much as I rock with her, I think being single is the move for me. I can do what I want, and I don't have to hear anybody's mouth about it. It works for now."

I didn't have a problem with that. What I did have a problem with was possibly getting attached to this man and then him and her getting back together. It was obvious that he loved her. Against my better judgement, I decided to just go with the flow. Whatever happened, happened.

"So you never told me why you and your dude didn't really work out," Jovaughn stated, breaking my train of thought.

I shrugged my shoulders. "It just didn't. We weren't really on the same page. He was ready to settle down and get married and live a life that I wasn't quite ready for. Maybe it wasn't that I wasn't ready, I just didn't want to marry him. I'm not even sure why," I stated in a low voice. Every time I thought about the fact that I broke Leonard's heart, it fucked with me.

"It be like that sometimes," Jovaughn stated casually as the waitress brought him the check over. "I'm trying to hit the strip club tonight. You wanna roll with me?"

I raised one eyebrow at him. "Really?" Most men didn't want to take their women friend to a strip club because they wanted to be able to flirt with and maybe even take someone from the club home. I wasn't against strip clubs. I'm not bi-sexual, but all the times I went to strip clubs, I had fun. That was the shit I was talking about. I wanted to fuck with somebody fun. Not a stick in the mud.

"Why not? I think it'll be fun," he stated with a devious grin on his face.

I grinned back. "I'm down."

* * *

"Fuuuckkkkk," I moaned with my eyes closed. Despite the fact that the room was spinning, what ole girl was doing to my pussy with her mouth had me on the brink of an orgasm that felt like it was going to be out of this world.

Yeah, I know. Despite me saying that I'm not bi-sexual, I still ended back up at Jovaughn's apartment with him and stripper named Desire. She was a pretty, thick, light-skinned chick and after five drinks and a few tokes of Jovaughn's blunt, when he whispered in my ear while grabbing my pussy through my jeans, I wasn't strong enough to deny him. He said it in a way like he was asking my permission. Not like he was telling me. He damn near begged me and wanting to make him happy, I obliged. After all, I wanted to live on the wild side, right?

"Eat that shit up," Jovaughn growled as he smacked Desire on the ass while pounding into her from behind.

He left the TV on so he could have some light to enjoy the two women in his bed. I opened my eyes and saw Desire's head moving back and forth as she sucked and licked on my pussy like a piece of fruit.

"Oh my gahhhhhhhhh," I screamed as I lifted my ass off the bed and exploded into her mouth. She latched onto my clit and wouldn't let go, and my legs started shaking. "Fuck!" My chest heaved up and down and I licked my lips as I tried to process what happened.

Again, I'm not gay, but I was super turned on when she came up and leaned down to give me a kiss. She snaked her tongue in my mouth while Jovaughn was still fucking her, and we kissed passionately and aggressively like long lost lovers. Jovaughn eased out of her, switched condoms, and when he slid his dick in me, I was in heaven. Me and Desire continued to kiss for a good three minutes while Jovaughn fucked me hard and fast. I was so aroused, that I came again. Right after my orgasm, Jovaughn snatched his dick out of me and pulled the condom off. That was our cue to suck and we tag teamed the dick. She deep throated and I sucked his balls until he exploded onto her breasts, and then I licked it off.

I was there, but it's like I was having an out of body experience. I was just that drunk. I was so drunk that after she left, I just lay there and fell asleep almost instantly. The next morning, the sound of Jovaughn's sleep-filled, raspy voice jerked me out of a hard sleep.

"What you want me to do ma? You want me to go to his school and talk to him? Don't even act like that, 'cus you're the reason I'm not in the house with y'all Shay. You put me out and then his bitch ass pops don't even care about him."

I frowned up my face at the pounding in my head. I had to pee bad as hell, my mouth was dry, and there was a horrible after taste in it. I was sure my breath smelled like shit, and I just wanted to go home. I slowly got out of bed while Jovaughn semi-argued with who I presumed was his ex. He looked over at me as I walked naked in the bathroom and quietly closed the door behind myself. I felt too damn bad to trip. A recollection of how much I drank and the events from the night before came flooding back to me, and I wasn't sure if I should be ashamed or pat myself on the back for doing some wild, adventurous shit. I found a bottle of mouthwash and gargled. I then washed my face and went back into the bedroom to get dressed. By that time, Jovaughn was off the phone.

"How you feel?" he asked.

"Like shit," I mumbled with a slight laugh. I eyed the three condoms sprawled on his bedroom floor.

"Word? You was throwing that Henny back like a G. Listen, I gotta shoot out to my ex's son's school. He acting up and shit. I don't have the time to get you breakfast or nothing, so here. My treat." He pulled a hundred-dollar bill from his jean's pocket and handed it to me.

I gave him a small smile. "Thank you." My stomach was doing a low rumble, and I knew if I didn't eat soon, I'd be even sicker than I already felt. I said my good-byes and fled his apartment hoping that Alex wouldn't see me. Looking at my phone I saw that it was nine am. As I pulled out of the parking lot I thought about what I wanted to eat. I also thought about how Jovaughn already had me wrapped around his finger so soon. With Leonard, I enjoyed being in a situation where the man loved me more than I loved him. It seemed cruel, but you get the upper hand that way, and you're less likely to get hurt. As if I could predict the future, it's like I could already see me losing myself in Jovaughn, but I was headed for destruction full speed ahead and wasn't even trying to pump the brakes.

## PANAMA

"Game nigga," I panted as I bounced the ball in Jay's direction. We'd just finished a game of basketball and naturally, I whooped his ass.

We walked over to the bleachers, sat down and picked up our bottles of water. Working out or playing ball was a stress reliever for me. I'd never be able to fully relax until Quadim was dead. There was also a slight nagging feeling in my gut because I'd sold all the heroin that Castillo gifted me with, and now I was just selling weed. Selling drugs was risky period, but the fact that I was doing so while on papers was even riskier. Still, a nigga had to eat.

"What you out here doing?" Jay asked, and I looked over at him curiously.

"What you mean?"

"I'm not trying to get in your business but you just came home right? Do you work? 'Cus you don't look like you're hurting for money." Before I could answer, he held his hands up in surrender. "Again, I'm not trying to get in your business, and I'm not judging, but I told you before if you need help, I got you. I meant that."

I furrowed my brows. "Help me how though?"

"Maybe a job or something. I'm not just a lawyer. I own a heating and air conditioner repair business with my father and I also own a tow truck business. If you want to do the HVAC business my company will send you to school and pay for the certification. Also, if you wanted to do the tow truck, we'd pay for you to get your CDL's. The HVAC pays some damn good money. I'm just putting that out there. You don't have to make a decision right now."

"Wow, I really appreciate that." Jay was cool and I knew he said he appreciated the way I stuck up for him in school, but I was still surprised by his offers. He really was offering me a way out. That HVAC shit was probably some long hours and not so easy work, but I was a man before anything. I wouldn't let hard work intimidate me. Standing on the block or even trapping in my car was easy and fast and so was that money, but the time wasn't worth it. Like the true hustler that I was, I even thought about working for him and selling weed on the side. That was as good as having two jobs. I knew Alex said she didn't need me to take care of her, but it was my nature to want to have her living good. Shit, it wasn't even just about her, I wanted to live good my damn self.

"It's no problem man. Like I told you, I got you."

The entire drive home, I thought about what he had proposed. When I got in, Alex was sitting at her vanity flat ironing her hair. I walked over to her and kissed her on the cheek where her newfound dimple was. She hated it, but I told her it added to her beauty. "Guess what?" I asked, and she looked at me through the mirror.

"What's up?"

I told her what Jay had offered me and by the time I was done talking, she'd turned all the way around to face me. "Babe are you serious? That's awesome Panama. Are you going to do it?" She was so excited, that I almost didn't want to her tell her that I wanted to, but I wasn't exactly sure when.

"I really want to do the HVAC joint, but that requires school for at least four months. I kind of want to get off some of this work first. Stack my bread a lil' bit. You about to start school too. Both of us can't be in school full-time."

Alex let out a defeated sigh. "Panama, please don't take too long okay?" Her eyes held a hint of worry. "This is a great opportunity. Don't worry about me being in school. I keep telling you that I got my packaging in today for my cleansers and moisturizers, and until school starts I'm going to spend my days mixing up stuff. I maxed out a credit card ordering everything that I need in bulk."

I reached in my pocket and pulled out all the money that I'd made for the day. I placed it on the vanity. "Pay that shit off. Now. I don't need you maxing out your credit cards. For as much as you tell me not to do everything, I'm still gon' look out for you. That's the whole point of me being out here risking my freedom."

Alex stood up. "That's just it. I don't want you risking your freedom. You have a golden opportunity here, and I need you to take it Panama. Please."

I kissed her on the lips. "I am. I promise."

My cell phone rang, and concern immediately covered my face when I saw that my grandmother from Panama was calling. She called me at least twice a month, but something about seeing her name on my phone screen put me on alert.

"Hey Nana," I answered.

"Panama if you can, I need you to come as soon as you can. Your father had a heart attack, and he's been unresponsive for the past three hours. You may have to come and say your good-byes."

## ALEX

I stood in my kitchen measuring ingredients for the first batch of skin care products that I was going to make. I knew that business might start off slow, but I still didn't want to start with little inventory. My website was being created, and I was going to do an official launch once I had at least sixty bottles made. I prayed that it wouldn't take me long to sell out. I also knew that school would take up most of my time, so I wanted to get plenty bottles made. Once school did start, I would only make products on the weekends. I'd spent hours researching skin care, reading about it, and experimenting with what really worked versus what didn't. If I was able to make $500 a month profit, I'd be happy. As long as Panama was paying the bills, I'd stack my money. In the event that he did stop hustling to go to school, I wanted to be able to take care of us. I got so tired of trying to beat it in his head that he didn't have to do everything by himself.

He'd been in Panama for a day, and his dad had regained consciousness, but it was still touch and go. I hoped that everything would be okay. The doorbell rang, and I knew it was Natalia. I never minded her coming over, but the fact that she stopped by once a day just to check Jovaughn's snap was sick to me. I could tell she liked his ass, and I hoped it didn't come back to bite her in the ass. I knew Jovaughn's type, and more than likely he didn't mean her any good, but she would have to find that out on her own. It didn't take a rocket scientist to know that Natalia was feeling the hell out of his thugged out ass. He was a big change from Leonard. I know people like what they like and honestly, a lot of women had a bad boy fetish, and that fetish was often their downfall. Look at me and Quadim.

"What's up?" I asked as I let her in the apartment.

"Not much. I came bearing gifts." She held up a plastic bag, and I could see the bag contained two bottles of wine.

"Oh okay. I'm in the kitchen cooking up some new stuff. Grab some glasses. Did you try that sample I gave you?" I handed her my phone because I already knew what she wanted, and she laughed.

"Thank you, and yes I did. That shit had my face soft as hell. I think you're onto something boo."

"If only I could get a big company to back me and put my shit in stores. Once I start seeing some money, I can afford the really good, high-end ingredients. For now, this will just have to do."

Natalia removed the bottles from the bag, opened them, and poured two glasses of wine. "Well, I think what you have now works wonders. A lot of people are wanting natural and organic products. In time, I think you'll do fine. It's just going to take a lot of advertising, and maybe giving out at least a hundred free samples. You got this though," she encouraged me.

"Thank you," I stated as I took the glass of wine from her. I hoped it would calm my nerves and keep my mind from worrying about Panama.

Natalia began her routine of looking through my phone. I could hear Jovaughn's voice, and he sounded all loud and animated. Then I heard music. Natalia was all in the phone watching intently. I didn't even know why she kept doing it to herself. Most times, she ended up seeing shit that pissed her off, but as I always reminded her, Jovaughn wasn't her man. "What's going on?" I asked after a few minutes. She wasn't saying shit, so I knew that was a bad sign.

Natalia ignored me for a second, then she looked up at me. "This nigga is in Cancun with the Incredible Hulk. I just talked to him two days ago, and he didn't say shit to me about going on a trip."

A light snicker escaped my lips, and I observed the distraught expression on Natalia's face. "I'm not laughing at you, it's just crazy how you call that girl the Incredible Hulk. Natalia, stop doing this to yourself. He already told you that they have a crazy bond right? That's nigga talk for I love her, and she not going nowhere. Now, he told you that so you could decide if you wanted to go or if you wanted to stay. You chose to stay, so you gotta take what comes with that baby girl."

"I know," she mumbled. "It's just not fair. He takes me out at least once a week. He's given me money twice. We never go more than two days without talking. He sexes me crazy. I just, it's just hard not to like him. But I have to like him knowing that he loves someone else."

I chose not to respond. I always try to think of how she didn't judge me when I was stupid and didn't leave Quadim when I should have. It was just hard to look at her and know that she gave up a good man to chase a nigga like Jovaughn. He was honest with her about the Incredible Hulk and in my eyes, he got major cool points for that. I just didn't see him settling down with her and giving her the good, stable life that Leonard would have. She looked so pitiful as she sipped her wine that I had to say something.

"Maybe it's her birthday or something. The trip was probably planned way before he even knew you. Don't read too much into it. Just live your life like the single, carefree, independent woman that you are, and don't worry about anything. Okay?"

That got a smile out of her. "Works for me. I need you to blow up with your skin care line so I can come work for you and quit that fuck ass job at Amazon. I see myself cursing one of the customers out one day and losing my job."

I laughed as my phone rang. I was thinking it might be Panama, but it was my other cousin. "Hey," I answered the phone before placing my wine goblet to my lips.

"It's time."

# QUADIM

"Nice crib," I stated as I entered Robin's house. She lived in a house in a nice neighborhood about thirty minutes from me.

"Thank you." She smiled at me before walking over to her grey leather couch. Shorty's ass was so damn phat that I was mesmerized. I wasn't sure if I'd ever fucked a female with a body as sick as hers, and I'd had sex with plenty of women. I sat down beside her as she picked up a cup filled with dark liquor.

"Let me get some of that," I stated as I pulled weed and cigars from my coat pocket. I was gon' get good and fucked up and fuck the shit out of her.

"Okay." She stood up and headed for the kitchen. I watched her ass until it was out of sight. "Got damn," I mumbled to myself as I took the wrap off the cigar.

Robin came back a few minutes later and handed me my cup. "Thanks."

"You're welcome."

We talked about what she was watching on TV while I rolled up. Once I was done, I pulled a lighter from my pocket and set fire to the end of the blunt. I inhaled deeply and enjoyed that first toke as weed smoke traveled through my lungs. I held the shit in for a minute before exhaling. I then hit the blunt two more times and passed it to her. The ice in my drink didn't do anything to take away the potency. I could for sure drink Henny straight without blinking, but the shit was strong as fuck. After five or six sips, I felt mellow as fuck and horny too. Robin passed me the blunt back, and I looked at her with hooded eyes. "Come over here shawty." I licked my lips, ready to slide up in between those thick ass thighs.

She looked over at me with red eyes and a grin. "You want me to come over there? What you gon' do with all this when I get over there?"

"You gon' find out shawty. I'm not even with all the talking."

She leaned in and placed her lips on mine. I held the blunt between two fingers as our wet, Henny coated tongues did a dance. My dick got rock hard in a matter of seconds. We broke the kiss, and she stood up as I picked my cup back up and took a few more large sips. As she sat her massive ass on my lap straddling me, my eyelids got heavy as fuck, and I had to fight to keep them open. I hadn't taken a pain pill since then, and I thought it would be out my system. It must not have been because the sips of Henny that I consumed were the amount of maybe two shots. The blunt wasn't even halfway gone. My tolerance level was way higher than that.

Robin began kissing on my neck, and my hands rested on the dip in her back. No matter how hard I fought, I couldn't keep my eyes open, and I nodded off while she was kissing and licking on me. I didn't know how long I was out for, but when I woke up, the first thing I noticed was that my hands were in front of me bound together with duct tape. My feet were taped as well. I still felt groggy as hell, but my head flew up and my eyes scanned the room. "What the fuck?" I panicked as I saw Robin sitting in a recliner smoking a blunt, just staring at me. The first thought that slammed into my brain was that this bitch was trying to set me up to be robbed. Snake ass bitch. "You fuckin' drugged me," I accused as she smiled. I wanted to slap the shit out of her ass. Fuckin' bitch. "If you thought I brought money with me, you bugging. I'd never bring money with me to a hoe's house. I came to stuff dick in you and then be out," I snarled at her. "If some lil' niggas think they gon' rob me, they're wasting their time."

"I give a fuck about your money."

My chest tightened when I heard that voice. It wasn't Robin's. I looked to my left and saw Alex walking into the living room with a sick grin on her face. She was gon' kill the fuck out of me. I could see it in her eyes. She was still beautiful as ever. Me shooting her in the face did nothing to change that fact. In some strange way, she looked even better, and like a sucka, I found myself wishing that shit could have been way different. I was gon' die and leave Quashon all alone in the world when it was never supposed to be like that. I didn't want to grovel like a punk, but got damn, it wasn't supposed to end like this. Alex walked over to me and I could damn near see the fire blazing in her eyes.

"You shot me three times and left me for dead. Maybe you thought Castillo was looking for you. Maybe you even suspected that Panama would come for you, but nah bitch, this beef is personal. From the start, all I ever did was love yo' pathetic, deranged, demonic, bitch ass. Even though you aren't capable of loving anyone else, I still loved you. Still stayed with you after countless bruises and ass whoopings, and that wasn't even enough for you. You really tried to murder me." Alex looked hurt, and she had every reason to be.

I spoke up, hoping that just maybe she'd have a change of heart. "It wasn't all bad Alex, and I know you know that I did love you. I had a fucked up way of showing it. I can admit that. But you left me and immediately got with the next nigga. That shit broke my heart yo," I confessed. It did. Knowing that she was with Panama killed me on the inside.

"Ohhhhh okay, I get it. I don't want to be with you anymore, so you just kill me. Oh okay." Alex nodded her head. "Thing is, I didn't die, hoe." She turned towards Robin. "You got that?"

"Yeap." Robin stood up and Alex turned back towards me.

"You never met my cousin from Virginia, huh? This is Robin. Thick right? I knew you'd be a sucka for a fat ass. See here's the thing, the bitch you were fucking, Lynn? Yeah. She came to the hospital to see me. Said she didn't know how sick and twisted you really were, and she gave up your location. I sat in that hospital bed and plotted like a muhfucka, and when Robin told me she was moving to town, I knew that it was my lucky break. I got her to follow you to the gas station that day and put herself in your line of vision. I knew everything else would fall into place. See even though he's careful, I don't want my nigga getting caught up behind you. I'm gon' do this shit myself."

Even though my life was on the line, it pissed me off to hear her refer to Panama as her nigga. I had it bad for Alex, but I was never able to show it in the right way. "So you care more about that fuck nigga than me? Yeah I shot you, I fucked up, but you really gone disregard everything I did for you? When I met you, you were walking. I put you in a whip. I got you out your mom's crib. I put food in your belly, and you said fuck me for that nigga? Why? 'Cus he on Castillo dick now?"

Alex eyed me with pure disgust written all over her face. "You are so stupid it should be a crime. It's not about what he bought me, it's about how he treated me. That bid was hard, and I didn't ride it out with him, but that was my fault. I wouldn't care if Panama was dirt broke, he's more of a man than you will ever be. He knows how to get his point across without putting his hands on me or calling me out my name. He knows how to treat me. I couldn't care less if he never bought me another thing ever in life. I'm still gon' suck the soul out his ass every night. I'll deep throat that nigga 'til the sun comes up."

My nostrils flared from anger. She was really trying me and it's because she had me bound. I didn't care how froggy she was feeling.

Alex would never come at me like that if she didn't have the upper hand. "Can you just please let me go? I'll never bother you again. You have my word on that. You gon' let Quashon go to foster care? He didn't have nothing to do with me shooting you. I told him I just wanted to talk to you. Nigga cried like a baby after I did what I did. I'm all he has man."

Alex's upper lip curled into a snarl. "Well he doesn't have much."

She was really playing hard ball. That nigga had done got in her head. I mean, it was probably because I shot her too, but damn. The Alex I used to know never looked at me with such hatred. She was looking at me like seeing me take my last breath would make her have an orgasm or some shit. She was getting a lot of joy out of what was to come. Dealing in the streets, I left the house every day knowing I might not make it back. Just because I knew that death could very well be my reality at any moment, the thought of being moments away from death had a nigga sweating. I wasn't ready to go. I had more money to make and more pussy to get. Plus, I really didn't want my brother in the foster care system. I might have been a fucked up nigga but he had it better with me than he would most likely have in a home.

Robin came from the back with two syringes in her hand. "I have no idea how to mix heroin, so I got somebody to do it for me."

My eyes damn near jumped out of the socket. "Yoooo, heroin? What you about to do Alex? Come on man."

She looked at me with a smirk. "See this isn't Robin's house. It's an Airbnb. I can't shoot you or stab you and leave blood everywhere, so I'm going to make it look like an overdose. She's going to call 9-1-1 after you die and tell them that she had a friend over and while she was in the shower, you shot up some heroin and died. No one will ever suspect a thing."

This bitch was sick. She really had it all planned out, and her ass would never see a day in prison for what happened to me. My heart started pounding so loud that I could hear it in my ears. "Alex." My breath was short, and I damn near couldn't breathe. She was really about to kill me. "Alex, come on. You don't have to do this. Think about Quashon. He needs me." I was starting to panic.

Alex walked towards me, and I tried to jerk away, but I couldn't go far. Robin's hoe ass came up behind the couch that I was sitting on and put me in a head lock. For a bitch, she was strong as fuck, and I for sure couldn't get away from Alex. She tied a belt around my arm so she could find a vein. She was really going out of her way to try and make the shit look like a legit overdose. I'd never been religious in my entire life. After all, I was dealt a shitty hand. My life had been rough since as far back as I could remember. If God was so real, why did He let my mom do all that fucked up shit to me when I was little? I felt like it was pointless to go around praying to and idolizing a God that never did shit for me, but as I stared death in the face all I could do was pray. As I watched Alex stick the needle in my vein and push the syringe, I repented for all my sins. It would be crazy as hell if the afterlife was real and God welcomed me into the pearly gates.

Not even thirty seconds after she pushed the drug into my veins, euphoria took over my body. It felt as if I was floating, and I could immediately see why fiends spent their days chasing this shit. Even with knowing that I was about to die, I was so calm and at peace, the shit was surreal. My eyelids became heavy and little did Alex know, she'd done me a favor. This was a banging ass way to die, so the joke was for sure on her ass. Saliva dripped from my bottom lip as I went into a dope fiend nod and then my whole world went black.

# ALEX

I inhaled weed smoke as I tried to concentrate on what was playing on the television screen in front of me. It had been a whole twenty-four hours since I killed Quadim, and that shit was fucking with me something bad. After the first shot of heroin, he just went into a nod and he looked like he felt no pain, but after I shot him up the second time, he started seizing and foaming at the mouth. He died in front of me, and I didn't feel any type of joy or relief. Even after that man stood over me with a gun and shot me in the face, just knowing that I'd killed someone damn near gave me a panic attack. I left before Robin called 9-1-1, and I had a total and complete breakdown. The Bible says an eye for an eye, but I felt like some bad ass karma was going to come my way for taking a man's life, and it had me uneasy as hell. I was jumpy, and I was on edge. I had to take Tylenol PM just to go to sleep that night, and I still had a nightmare. I woke up crying and sweating.

Panama's dad was okay, and he was on his way home, and for that I was grateful. Since he was on papers, he wasn't even supposed to be out of the city, but he didn't give a damn. He wasn't coming back until his dad was okay. Even though Robin was there when I killed Quadim,

I still had to vent and get the shit off my chest. I needed to talk to someone, and the only other person I trusted with the information was Panama. When he opened that front door and walked into the apartment, I jumped into his arms so hard and fast I damn near knocked him down. I hugged him so tight that he chuckled.

"Damn ma, I missed you too."

I jumped out of his arms and looked at him. I wasn't exactly sure what kind of expression my face held, but Panama knew something was up. "What's good? Talk to me."

I grabbed his hand and led him over to the couch. Once we were seated, I told him everything. I told him about Robin, Lynn, me killing Quadim. I didn't hold anything back and when I was done talking, the look that Panama's face held was one of disbelief. "Alex, tell me you're lying."

"No. Quadim is dead. The nigga shot me and left me there. It was either him or me or you or him. I had the drop on him so I figured out a way to kill him so that no one would have to worry about going to prison. As much as I hate him, I had no idea that his death would haunt me like this."

"What if that shit had backfired? Huh?" Panama raised his voice, and it was unexpected, so I jumped a little. "That man already showed you that he didn't give a damn about killing you. What if he'd managed to get away from you? You don't do shit like that without me Alex. You gotta be smarter than that." Panama was pissed.

"Robin drugged him before I even got there. He was out of it. The nigga didn't even stir when we taped his hands and feet together. I wasn't in any danger."

Panama let out an angry chuckle. "You wasn't in any danger. Aight, I got you." He stood up and headed for the bedroom. He was in there for a good twenty minutes and then he left the apartment without saying good-bye or telling me where he was going. I let out a frustrated sigh. I had been waiting for hours on end for him to come home so I wouldn't have to be alone. I didn't expect him to get mad and leave like that. I really didn't see why he was so angry. Robin and I had the shit under control.

Once I was alone again, my thoughts roamed back to that night with Quadim. I just saw him convulsing. It wouldn't leave my mind. I heard a noise, and I jumped. It's as if I thought his evil ass was going to haunt me. When I took a shower, I left the bathroom door open. I was afraid of a damn ghost. Had I known I would suffer the way that I was, I would have left Quadim for Castillo and Panama to handle. After a few minutes of sitting alone on the couch, I got up and headed for the kitchen. I needed something that would put me out for the night, and I could only pray that I wouldn't have nightmares. I couldn't take back what I'd done, but I for sure would if I could.

I took something to help me sleep and then I headed for the bathroom to brush my teeth before bed. My nerves were so rattled I couldn't even be bothered with wondering when Panama was coming back. After I was ready for bed, I climbed in and turned on the television. I'd never be able to sleep in silence again. Closing my eyes, I begged God to forgive me for what I'd done. I wasn't even sure what I'd have to do to rectify that sin. Once I was done praying, I watched the movie that was playing while I waited on sleep to take over.

I wasn't sure exactly how long I'd been out, but I jumped slightly when I felt lips on the back of my shoulder. I turned my head and Panama was in bed with me. The smell of Dove invaded my nostrils and then the shampoo that he used. I couldn't describe the smell but it's masculine. There was an apologetic look in his eyes. He didn't speak though, he just placed a soft kiss on my lips. He then got on top of me and our tongues did a tango. Before I knew it, I was gasping into his mouth as he was sticking his dick in my pussy. Panama sexed me like he missed me. He sexed me like he loved me. When we were done, he looked into my eyes.

"If anything ever happened to you, I'm not sure how I would handle it

Alex. When Butta called me and told me you were shot, my whole world stopped for a few minutes. I'm not even sure that I was breathing. I don't think you know how much I love you, and I just need you to make better decisions. Aight?"

I simply nodded my head. I'd only had three boyfriends in my life, and aside from family, no man had ever loved me the way Panama loved me. Whatever he said, I was with it. He kissed me again and wrapped his arms around me. I drifted off to sleep praying that the start of my new life would be enough to make me forget the horror of taking a man's life. First Quadim tormented my life, and now he was tormenting my soul. Something had to give.

# QUASHON

I sat on the bed in my brother's room staring in his closet. It had been two days since our aunt called me and told me she had to go identify my brother's body. Her number was on file from when Quadim was in the hospital once and listed her as an emergency contact. Our aunt was damn near fifty and not in the best health. Despite all that, her daughter still left three kids with her when she got locked up. The kids ranged in ages from ten to six. Her son, who was thirty, also lived there. That's five people in a two-bedroom, one-bathroom. I'd sleep from couch to couch before I went to live there.

I knew what she told me was some bullshit. I knew my brother, and he didn't overdose off no damn heroin. Someone had murdered him. They shot him up with the shit. Quadim didn't like popping pills, he never snorted shit, and he for damn sure wasn't using no heroin. With all the dirt he did though, I'd never know exactly who killed him. It could have been Panama, Butta, Castillo, or anybody. A few months before all the shit happened with Castillo and Panama, Quadim beat the fuck out of one of his workers because his money kept coming up short. It was safe to say more people hated my brother than loved him. His death wasn't a shock to me, but it still hurt.

It was the sixth of March, so the rent was paid. I had somewhere to stay for the rest of the month. I was officially on my own. Quadim had his fucked up ways, but I missed him. Since Alex left, he was all that I had in the world. God just kept taking people away from me, and it wasn't fair. Why didn't I deserve to be loved and to be happy? Why couldn't I be spoiled with a big family that loved me. I just didn't understand what I had done so wrong in my life.

Tired of moping, I stood up and went through his shit. Any drugs that he had, I would sell to get money. Any money that he had would go towards bills. I needed to be able to hold the house down for as long as I could. It took me an hour of going through all his shit, and I finally had one brick of heroin and $30,000 in cash. I was relieved because at least I wouldn't have to worry about finding somewhere to move any time soon. All I had to do was take the money order for the rent to the rental office and say I was Lynn's brother or some shit. The crib that we had was in her name. My aunt called the funeral home for me and made the arrangements. I was going to step up to the plate though. I was going to buy him a suit and some fly shoes to be buried in. Luckily, my aunt was good for something. She had an insurance policy out on Quadim, so his funeral was taken care of. I knew she only took one out on him because she knew he'd die young. Her money hungry ass was about to reap the benefits of my brother's death. I heard her ass trying to bargain and get the cheapest shit. Her policy was for $25,000 and she was trying to get him buried for around ten bands so she'd have plenty of change left over. Trifling ass bitch.

I began weighing and bagging up the heroin. I needed to keep my mind busy. It was three days before the funeral, and I was numb. I'd been going to see my son every day. Being a father was growing on me. Yeah, I was young, but I knew I never wanted my son to grow up and feel alone the way I felt my whole life. It had become a routine for me to watch him for an hour or two so Ebony could do homework, do laundry, wash his bottles, catch a nap, or whatever it was that she needed to do. I didn't mind. He was a good baby. If he was awake, he'd just stare up at me like my face was the most interesting thing in the world to him. A tear rolled down my cheek as I realized that I never even got to tell Quadim that he was an uncle. I stopped bagging up the heroin, broke down, and cried. My muhfuckin' nigga was gone man.

* * *

I narrowed my eyes as a red Camry pulled up in front of the house. I was sitting outside on the porch smoking a blunt. I'd smoked a few times, but it wasn't anything that I did on a regular basis. After everything I'd been through though, I deserved to roll up. Quadim had a nice little stash in the house. Cigars too. I exhaled weed smoke and watched as Ebony got out of the driver's side of the car. "I've been calling you. Why haven't you answered?"

I shrugged. "Haven't looked at my phone." It was the day of my brother's funeral. I didn't even go to the gravesite. A good sixty people attended the funeral. A bunch of his old hoes showed up, niggas from the neighborhood, a few family members. I hadn't looked at my phone in about five hours.

"I know today was Quadim's funeral. I'm sorry Quashon. I know we weren't always on the best terms, but you really stepped up and been there for me and Tristan. I appreciate that."

"It's no problem," I mumbled and hit the blunt again.

She sat down beside me. "So you just gon' stay here by yourself?" I nodded my head. "I told my mom what happened. She cooked today. There's a plate in the car if you want. She cooked turkey wings, rice and gravy, cabbage, and corn on the cob. She appreciates how you've been helping me too. She says I'm doing good and even though she wished I had still waited before having a baby, she's proud of us."

My stomach started to growl at just the mention of the food. I looked over at her. "Yeah that would be dope. Thanks. Tell your mom I said thanks." I didn't know how to cook shit but noodles and microwaveable stuff. I was really out here on my own. I couldn't even believe it.

"If you want, me and Tristan could come over and keep you company. Just so you won't have to be alone. You can take the couch, and we'll sleep in your bed." She nudged me playfully. "He still doesn't sleep through the night, so prepare to hear crying."

"Your moms will let you do that?" I asked.

Ebony kissed her teeth. "Boy, I'm grown. I already got a baby, what else can happen? I'm on birth control. I for sure won't be pushing another baby out anytime soon. Plus, my six weeks isn't even up. We couldn't have sex if I wanted to, and I don't want to. Taking care of a baby leaves me too tired to do anything."

"I don't want to have sex with you yo. I'd just appreciate if you and my son came and spent the night so I won't have to be alone. I haven't been sleeping much, so I can help you with him when he wakes up." I didn't care if I sounded like a punk. I was speaking the truth. Being in that house alone was torture.

"I got you. We're your family Quashon. You don't have to be alone. You're going to have to follow me back to my mom's though. She won't mind if we stay the night, but I for sure can't keep her car."

"That's cool. Can you bring me that plate first? I'm starving."

"Sure."

Ebony stood up, and I watched her walk to the car. The fact that she said her and Tristan were my family made me damn near smile. It literally felt like in the past few days a wall of ice had formed around my heart, but I had to have a soft spot for my son. Like she said, he was my family, and if she considered herself my family too, I'd take that. I needed all the people in my corner that I could get. I vowed that from that day forward, it would be just me, Ebony, and my baby.

## NATALIA

"Thank God for good weave." I giggled as Jovaughn and I headed for the waiting Uber. We were in Miami and had just gotten off jet skis, and my hair was soaked. I hadn't had that much fun in a long ass time.

Jovaughn was still Jovaughn. I'd finally gotten to the point where I didn't even desire to watch his snaps anymore. I'd come to the conclusion that he and Hulk would do what they did, but I just had to be worried about myself. The nigga had to be seeing major bread in the streets, because one day he just up and asked me if I wanted to come to Miami with him. Of course I said yes, and we'd been having a ball for the past two days. I damn near hated to go home. Our first day there, we ate at a nice ass restaurant, and the tab came to damn near three hundred dollars. Then we hit the mall, and Jovaughn bought me a fuckin' three thousand-dollar Chanel bag without blinking. That night we hit the strip club, we got fucked up, and I engaged in another threesome. I was only doing them for him, but I couldn't front like the shit didn't feel good as hell when I was partaking in them.

We'd been eating good, having fun, and just living life. My face was damn near hurting from smiling so much. Another awesome thing about the trip was that Jovaughn rented an Airbnb. He wanted to be able to smoke and shit in peace. We were staying in a nice ass four-bedroom, three-bathroom house with a pool in the back yard, in a very nice neighborhood. Jovaughn's ass had money, money, and I was here for it. He was the one that bought me the "good weave" before the trip, and that shit was six hundred dollars for three bundles and a frontal. Leonard was a good ass provider, but Jovaughn took the shit to another level. With me now working full-time, I was able to pay all of my bills on my own, but the extra money that he put in my pocket and the shit he did for me, helped a whole lot. It may seem materialistic as fuck, but after he bought me that Chanel bag, he deserved a threesome. Shit.

"That shit better be good for as much as it cost." He ran his fingers through the soaked curls. "We can grab some takeout, go in, eat, take a shower, then get dressed to hit the strip. It's our last night. We gotta turn up."

"Okay."

The house we were staying in was about twenty-five minutes away from the beach. By the time we got our food and got back to the house, I was famished. I had to take a shower first though. I ran upstairs to take a quick shower. While I waited on the water to warm up, I smiled at my reflection in the mirror. I was truly happy. Like happy for real. That's all I wanted in my life was some adventure tied to some good D, and the fact that the nigga had long paper didn't hurt either. In my eyes, I was winning. I didn't even care that Jovaughn wasn't my man. Everything didn't have to be about titles. I made sure I was good and clean, but I took a quick shower and washed my hair fast as hell, because the rumbling in my belly was getting louder and louder. Once I was out of the shower, I dried off, put lotion on my entire body, and threw a fitted tank top on with some boy shorts and headed downstairs. I was four steps away from the last step when I heard Jovaughn talking, and I immediately knew that he was on the phone. I then heard a female's voice. I'd seen enough snaps to know what the Incredible Hulk sounded like, so I knew it wasn't her. "I'm saying. I know you out of town and all but you can't pick up when I call?" she asked in a squeaky voice that irritated my soul. It had a dragging your fingernails across a chalkboard effect.

"I'm saying ma, if I told you I'm on vacation, I would assume that you'd know not to blow me up. I'm not thinking about no phone, and when you call me back to back like that the shit gets mad annoying."

"Well excuse me for wanting to talk to you. Vacation or not, it only takes a few minutes to say hello. You with a female?" she inquired, causing Jovaughn to let out a light chuckle.

"Shorty you doing a lot right now. I've known you what, a month? I made it clear from the beginning that I'm single. Don't ask me no whole bunch of questions that don't have anything to do with you. That shit is a turn off."

It was her turn to let out a chuckle. "Wow. Okay, well the last thing I want to do is turn you off. Holla at me when you get back Jovaughn."

"Will do."

So, there was me, Incredible Hulk, and Squeaky Voice. It's not like I felt like Jovaughn was a saint, but it was becoming more and more clear to me that no matter how much I liked this man, I'd never have him to myself. I wondered if I could really put up with that. You know, as humans, we always want to have our cake and eat it too, and Jovaughn had all the qualities that I wanted in a man. I just wanted him to worship the ground that I walked on like Leonard did, but that would probably never happen. He and Leonard were two very different types of people.

I counted to twenty in my head before going into the living room because I didn't want him to know that I'd heard his conversation. The trip had been fun and unproblematic so far, and I wanted to keep it that way. Jovaughn looked up as I walked into the room. "I like your hair curly like that. You should wear it like that more often."

"I'll keep that in mind."

Jovaughn and I discussed our plans for our last night in Miami, and in no time at all the conversation that I heard between him and Squeaky Voice was forgotten.

* * *

The next day, I was in the car with Jovaughn. We had gotten back from Miami, and he was driving to his apartment complex so he could stop by home and so I could get my car. I was tired and nestled deep in the leather seat enjoying the ride and ready to see my bed. It had been a fun-filled past few days with little to no sleep, and my body was exhausted. My thumb moved upwards as I scrolled through Instagram. I damn near scrolled past a picture that made me do a double take, and I lifted the phone just a bit because I felt like I had to be tripping. Leonard rarely ever posted on IG so even after we broke up, I hadn't even thought to unfollow him. It was my first time seeing him post since our break-up, and what I was staring at made my heart pound hard in my chest. "This motherfucker," I mumbled. Thankfully, Jovaughn didn't hear me because he had the music turned up loud as hell.

I stared at the picture not believing what I was seeing. He had to be posting it just to get back at me because there was no way. He had posted a picture of him and a female at a resort in Jamaica, but it wasn't just any female. It was Robin! Robin wasn't my cousin, she's Alex's cousin on her dad's side, but I didn't give a damn. Every time she used to come down for the summer all of us used to hang out. Aside from commenting on each other's shit on social media, I hadn't spoken to her in person in about a year. I hadn't even seen her since she'd moved to North Carolina, but my ex should have still been off limits to her. Robin was going against the grain like a muhfucka. My nostrils flared from anger as I stared at the phone. The bitch was smiling like she was the happiest woman in the world, and Leonard's dumb ass couldn't even see that he was an easy mark. There was no way that Robin liked him for real.

That bitch was hood as hell, and all she'd ever dated was dope boys and murderers. She dated niggas more along the lines of Quadim. She'd been in a relationship a few years back where she used to get her ass beat too. She finally left the dude after he beat her and made her lose the baby she was carrying at the time. I continued to scroll, and I saw more pictures of their little baecation. He had posted a picture of her sitting on a huge rock in a black two-piece, and for as mad as I was, I couldn't even front; her body was to die for. Her body was sicker than mine, and she was natural; meanwhile, I'd had work done.

There was also one of her cheesing and smiling all damn wide and hard at a pool party in a different swimsuit. This one was a one-piece, but it was Versace, and she had on some Versace slides and shades. I knew good and damn well, Leonard wasn't cashing out on Versace; he hadn't worked that much overtime. Plus, he had good credit, but he wasn't doing it like that to be maxing out cards on designer shit. The most expensive thing he'd ever bought me was some $800 Louboutin heels, and he worked overtime for two months to pay the shit off his card. Leonard made decent money, but he was far from a baller. Robin was that kind of hood chick that played cards and shot dice, smoked weed, popped pills, got drunk as hell, partied every weekend, like what in the fuck would Leonard want with her?

He had to just be trying to make me mad. After all, I hadn't posted Jovaughn on my page, but I'd definitely posted plenty of pictures from Miami. Being that I didn't post a female, he probably assumed that I was with a man. I had almost calmed myself down when I came across a picture that made my blood boil. It was a picture of Robin carrying a bag from the Louis Vuitton store, and the caption read: *what she wants she gets.*

My mouth damn near fell open in shock. This man was really about to go broke trying to make me jealous. Maybe it wasn't to make me jealous, maybe it was to try and ease the pain from our break-up, but if he thought I hurt him, I hoped he was prepared to get played like hell by

Robin. We pulled up in front of Jovaughn's building, and I looked around the parking lot in search of Alex's car to see if she was home.

"I had fun," Jovaughn stated as he cut his car off.

"Me too. I'll call you later." I leaned over and gave him a kiss on the lips. He got out of the car, popped the trunk and got my bags out.

After I put my bags in my car, I headed towards Alex's building and climbed the stairs to her floor. I had half a mind to call him, but I didn't want to do so while he was with her. If he wanted to move on that was fine, but he didn't have to do it with someone that I knew. I rang Alex's bell, and she answered a few seconds later. "Hey. When did you get back?" she greeted me with a small, white, furry puppy in her hand.

"When did you get a dog?" I asked stepping inside of the apartment.

"Yesterday. Panama got her for me. Isn't she the prettiest little thing?" Alex smiled at the puppy.

"Adorable," I stated in a sarcastic tone. "So you weren't going to tell me that your hoe ass cousin was fucking with Leonard?" I asked with an obvious attitude.

The smile left Alex's face instantly. "Nah, I wasn't going to tell you because it wasn't my place. I take it you saw the Instagram pictures?"

I jerked my head back. "It wasn't your place? You're my blood Alex, and that's foul. So how long have you known? Ain't this some shit? Robin is foul as fuck, and you know it."

"You're foul too, but did I tell Talisha about you and my dad? Even when she called me calling herself going off on me, I checked her ass and haven't spoken to her since. Both of y'all are my cousins. I told Robin it was wrong, and she said she doesn't owe you any loyalty. If you feel some kind of way talk to her, but don't come up in here bucking at me. I have my own problems, and at the end of the day I get tired of being thrown in the middle of shit that has nothing to do with me. You shit on Leonard, so he's for damn sure not caring about your feelings. He tried to holla at her, and she was with it. Despite how I felt."

"You love hollering about how I did Leonard wrong, and how you're team him, but you think she likes him? You know good and well Robin is using his gullible ass. Have you given her any speeches?"

"Nah I haven't, because she told me she really likes him. Again, I don't have anything to do with any of it."

"You know what, I don't even give a fuck," I stated as I turned and walked out the door. Fuck Alex. Fuck Leonard. Fuck Robin.

# ALEX

## ONE YEAR LATER...

I sighed as I looked over at the clock and closed my textbook. I was tired, and I couldn't hold my eyes open any longer. It was almost two in the morning, and I was pissed off. Panama had gotten back from being out of town on business. He was supposed to be back around eight pm, and he still hadn't made it in. I hadn't seen him in four days, so you would have thought that his first stop would have been home, but of course not. I was mad about a lot of shit. I was mad that despite Jay's offer, Panama still hadn't taken the HVAC class, and he still wasn't working a legal job. In fact, he was deep in the drug game. He still only sold weed, but he was moving major weight, like around six hundred pounds a month. The nigga was hardly ever home, he had three phones that rang damn near non-stop, and it was my worst fear that he was going to go back to prison. He seemed to have forgotten everything he said about being done with the streets.

Just as I was about to go to the bedroom, Panama walked through the front door carrying a duffel bag and looking tired. "What's up bae?" he asked as he walked over towards me, and I shot him daggers with my eyes.

"You've been back in town for how many hours, and you're just now getting in? It's nice to know how much of a priority I am." My voice was thick with attitude. I folded my arms underneath my breasts and waited for some bullshit to spew from his lips.

Panama kissed his teeth. "Alex, please don't start. You already know how this shit goes. What good is me going out of town to get drugs if I'm not going to start selling them as soon as I get back? I be having niggas waiting on me to get back in town. I make them wait too long and they go get the shit from someone else. They don't cop from me, then I don't make money."

"That's the whole fucking problem Panama. You weren't supposed to be doing this shit long term. You have an offer for a damn good job. The man is even willing to send you to school, and you may as well have spit in his face! That was a year ago!"

Panama dropped his duffel bag on the floor and spoke between clenched teeth. "And I told you that when I get ready to go to school, I'm going to fall back from hustling and in order to do that, my bread needs to be right."

"Nigga your bread is right now! I have access to your safe, or did you forget? Broke is one thing that you're not. Since you won't let me pay any bills, my bank account isn't too shabby. You can afford to quit now." It took about six months for my skin care products to really start making me some money. At first, I made around $200 a month, mostly from people I knew. After six whole months of sponsoring ads on social media, networking, giving out free samples, and word of mouth from my customers, month six was the month that I made $1,800 and I was shocked and excited. That just gave me motivation to go even harder. I invested $1,500 of that right back in the company and month seven I made $3,500. My biggest month so far, I'd made $9,400. I was getting orders in faster than I could make the products. I had to dedicate at least two days a week, eight hours out of the day to making the creams and packaging them.

"I appreciate your concern Alex, but I got this."

"Do you? Because you're not invincible. You can't control whether or not you get arrested, and—"

He rudely cut me off. "And we know that if I go back to prison, you for damn sure ain't gonna do a bid with me."

He walked towards the back, and I stood there stuck on stupid. That was some shit that he didn't even have to say, and I didn't even have a comeback for his ass. I stood there for about five minutes until I heard the shower come on. I then went in the bedroom and threw on some leggings, a tank top, and slid my feet into some PINK slides. I grabbed an overnight bag and packed an outfit, and I grabbed a few other things. I also went in the other bathroom and grabbed one of the spare toothbrushes that we kept in the house. After grabbing my bookbag and my dog, I headed outside towards my car. Panama had me fucked up.

I was just going to stay at my mom's house for the night to cool off. I had class the next day, and I wasn't trying to be up all night arguing. If I kept thinking about what he said to me, I might be tempted to slap fire out his ass. Panama could holler that he forgave me all he wanted to, but the truth of the matter was if he could get mad and say shit like that, then he wasn't over it. I had been slowly trying to get back to normal after killing Quadim, but that shit still nagged at me. I still saw his face with foam coming out of his mouth and him convulsing on that couch every single day. It was an image that I couldn't get out of my mind. On his birthday, I had a nightmare about that night, and I was crying in my sleep. It even woke Panama up.

I had a 4.0 GPA, and I was doing good in school. Keeping myself busy studying and trying to run a business was enough to keep me occupied most of the time, but it wasn't enough to make me forget. I also thought of Quashon every now and then. I would wonder where he was and if he was okay. Shit was crazy. If Panama did catch a charge and go back to prison, I for sure would hold him down this time. I was older and wiser, but if he didn't believe that I would, then I was done trying to convince him. I no longer had the energy or the desire to try and make him understand just how sorry I was.

*** 

The next day, I got out of class at three. I stopped by my mom's and picked the dog up. Her name was Lauren because Nipsey Hussle was my favorite rapper and since I didn't want to name a girl dog Nipsey, I named her after Nipsey's girl. When I got home, I saw Panama's Benz truck in his usual parking space. It was unusual for him to be home this time of the day unless he was just running in to grab a bite to eat, to pick something up, or drop money off. When I got inside of the apartment, he was sitting on the couch playing the game with a blunt hanging from his lips. He didn't even look up at me, so I headed for the bedroom.

"You not done with the stupid shit?" he called out, causing me to stop walking and turn around.

"Excuse you?"

"It took a lot for me not to find you last night and bring your ass home. I let you go vent, pout, cool off, or do whatever it is that you needed to do. So now are you ready to talk about this like a grown woman?"

I narrowed my eyes into slits and glared at him. He had a lot of nerve, but I bit the tip of my tongue, literally, and tried to speak with a calm voice. "You don't think you owe me an apology for what you said?"

Panama placed his controller on the coffee table and stood up. He walked over to me and stood directly in front of me. "I know I owe you an apology. I know I need to get my ducks in a row and chill on this street shit. I know all that." He looked down at me, and my breath caught in my throat. Despite me being mad at him, he was sexy as fuck, and it hit me that I was horny.

I didn't want to tell him that though. I wanted to be mad for just a little bit longer, so I attempted to walk away, but he pulled me back. "Don't do that Alex."

He kissed the corner of my mouth, and my body melted. He then gripped my chin in his hand and kissed my lips. Adding tongue, he kissed me with his usual passion. The way he kissed me always made me feel like he was hungry for me, and that shit made me wet as hell. He had me, and the anger melted off of me like snow in the sunshine. I'd much rather be wrapped in his arms than arguing. Panama and I were on the same page with that because he scooped me up and carried me to the bedroom. After we undressed, I took him into my mouth so I could show him just how much I missed him. His dick was exactly what I needed in my life.

My ass was tooted up in the air as I deep throated Panama's dick. He was on his back, so he positioned my pussy over his face and began to devour me. I moaned and hummed on his dick as he spread my pussy lips and slurped on me like I was something good to eat. The closer he brought me to an orgasm, the harder I sucked on his dick. My stomach caved in, and I still didn't stop sucking as I came all in Panama's mouth. I just moaned loudly with a mouth full of dick and slid my pussy up and down his lips.

He tapped me lightly on the ass, and that was my signal to get up. I turned around and straddled him, then I slid down on his dick as he licked his lips and moaned. I stared into his eyes, amazed at how he could piss me off one minute and have me crazy in love the next. "Come see how good your pussy tastes," he stated in a low voice as I leaned in and kissed him.

I sucked my essence off his tongue as I rode him slowly in an effort to prolong the ecstasy that he was giving me. The shit felt so good. "Give me six months, aight?" he asked in a low voice, and for a second, I was confused.

It dawned on me that he was talking about six more months in the game, and I just nodded my head. He could have said anything at that point, and I probably would have agreed. All I cared about at the moment, was his dick inside of me bringing me to the point of yet another orgasm. Panama was the love of my life, and I was riding with him right or wrong. Forever.

## PANAMA

"I never knew it was so pretty out here," Alex stated as she looked out of the window. I was taking her outside the city to a nice little subdivision that was being newly built. There was a huge lake in the back that would essentially be in everyone in the subdivision's back yard. There were twenty houses all being built and in different stages. None of the houses would be ready for another six months.

"Yeah, it's real nice out here," I stated, turning into the subdivision. Alex looked over at me.

"You riding through to see if any of the houses are going to be for rent?" she asked curiously.

I smiled. "Nah, I'm about to show you the joint that's being built that I'm going to own. Ain't no more renting shawty."

Alex's eyes widened with surprise. "Are you serious Panama? How are you buying a house?"

I pulled in front of what was soon to be our new home and put my car in park. "My homeboy is a lawyer with several legit businesses. For the past year, he's had me listed as an employee. I get check stubs, even got a few credit cards to help my credit. I only use them for shit like gas and food. Lil' shit. Then I wait about a week and just pay the shit off. I've been out here doing more than just running the streets ma. We got five bedrooms in that joint, three bathrooms, a theatre room, den, and living room. Plus, a three-car garage. You gon' have fun decorating this shit." I grinned at her. "I dropped fifty racks on this bitch. By the time it's finished, I'll have enough stashed to pay the mortgage for a year, and *then* I'll go to school and start working for Jay for real. Not to mention, I've invested in a weed dispensary out in Vegas."

Alex looked at me in amazement. "Just, wow. Why didn't you tell me any of this?"

I shrugged. "I wanted it to be a surprise. What do you think?"

She reached over and threw her arms around me. "I think you're amazing. I never doubted you; I just want you safe. That's all. I know you're smart. You're too smart to let it go to waste, but you got me eating my words. You seem to have it under control."

"Ahhhhh, that's what I'm talking about. Give me my props. I think I deserve some extra special head tonight too."

A sneaky grin slid across Alex's face. "Who says we have to wait until tonight?" She reached down inside of my basketball shorts and pulled my dick out.

I licked my lips in anticipation as she lowered her head and proceeded to give me some of the best head that I'd ever had in my life.

* * *

"Aye, you heard about Colby?" Butta asked me a few hours later.

Colby was one of my customers. In fact, I'd just sold him four pounds of weed the day before. "What about him?" I asked curiously.

"Nigga got knocked with four pounds of weed last night. He's in the county. So you already know if he got caught with four pounds, they gonna wanna know who his connect is. They don't want his lil' charge; they'd rather be able to get way more than that, feel me? You think he solid?"

I looked out of my car window as I contemplated Butta's question. My gut and first instinct told me hell nah. Colby was a pretty boy that liked to act like he was street, but I could see right through that shit. Nigga wouldn't last two days in prison, and that told me everything that I needed to know. "Not really."

"Me either. You know what that means right? I know you have a plan in place, but I think you should shut down shop for a few months. Go ahead and enroll in your class. Tell your clientele that you outta commission for a lil' bit, and if Colby calls you, don't answer the phone."

I nodded my head because even though I wasn't ready to interrupt my money flow at the moment, what Butta was saying was making sense. I couldn't be for sure if Colby would mention my name, and the last thing I needed was them boys watching me and trying to build a case. Like Alex said, I wasn't broke. Fact of the matter was, I was being a little greedy, but that money was addictive. Once you see how fast and plentiful it comes, it's hard to stop. It's like that with any kind of fast money. That's why most strippers stripped for years on end before they quit. Jack boys, hustlers, scammers, anybody that made fast money became hooked on the shit and even when they knew they need to stop, most times they didn't, and that greed was what got them caught every time.

As if our conversation had conjured him up, my phone rang, and it was Colby. I showed Butta the phone, and he shook his head. "Yeah, if that nigga just made bond and the first thing he wants to do is call you, then I wouldn't trust it. *If* he even made bond yet."

I watched the phone until it stopped ringing. Not even five seconds later, Colby was calling me right back. I once again watched it ring. "I think I'm about to get a new number right now."

I'd come too far to go back to prison. I wasn't making any more plays until further notice. If the police did decide to watch me, all they would see was a nigga going to class. That's it. Plus, despite Jay having me on his payroll, if I caught a drug charge and got a large amount of money confiscated from me, anything in my name like my house, the feds could look into and possibly take that shit. That thought alone was enough to scare me straight. The remaining weed that I had was in a climate-controlled storage unit inside glass jars. It would be good until I decided I wanted to sell weed again. For the moment, I was about to chill out though. Castillo was one of the most careful niggas I knew. He'd been selling heroin without so much as a petty charge for years but about two days before Alex killed Quadim, while I was still in Panama, he got picked up by the feds. I checked on him through his people and heard that he had a mean ass Jewish lawyer that was connected like a muhfucka. Even with his lawyer, he still got two years, which for a nigga like Castillo was a sweet ass deal because that nigga had served enough dog food to get him a life sentence. When he got caught though, I heard his driver was of course in the car, and Castillo talked his driver into taking the charge for the drugs. The police knew that the drugs belonged to Castillo, but when you have a grown man confessing to the shit, what can you do?

In exchange for half a million dollars, the driver ate the charge and got ten years. Castillo gave the money to his driver's wife, and her and the kids were out here living like royalty, and Simon was in prison living as best he could with $200 a week being put on his books. The police wanted Castillo so bad that they hit him with conspiracy and anything else they could. Two years was all the state was gon' get out of him though, and Castillo was going to come home and still be the man. He had an idea that maybe it was Quadim that rolled on him, but since Quadim was dead, he'd never know for sure. If a man as well connected and powerful as Castillo could still get hit with two years, I didn't want to be arrested again for shit.

Alex would be happy to know that for the moment, my hustling days had come to an abrupt halt. I dropped Butta off at my mom's crib and headed to get some gas, cigars, and something to drink before heading in for the day. Once I was settled at the crib, I'd call Jay and tell him that I was ready to register for the next available class at the community college. When I came out of the store, I had my head down looking at my phone, but I felt eyes on me. My street instincts kicked in, and I looked up. Quashon was leaning against Alex's old red Benz, and he was eyeing me. There were two Styrofoam cups in his hand, one stacked inside the other. Most times when people double stacked Styrofoam cups, it's because they're drinking lean. Sprite mixed with promethazine cough syrup. Lil' nigga had gone through a growth spurt or something. He looked way taller and even had a little peach fuzz on his chin. I wasn't feeling the way the nigga was eyeballing me. He had a slight scowl on his face like my presence irritated him. If he was old enough to feel like he wanted to try me, then I had no problem sending him to hell with his brother, so if he knew what was good for him, he'd better tread light.

# NATALIA

I logged into Alex's snapchat, and what I saw pissed me off so bad, I damn near busted a blood vessel. Yeah, a whole year later and my dumb ass was still checking Jovaughn's snap. This bitch ass nigga had me at his crib watching Incredible Hulk's son while he was out with the next bitch. Well, he wasn't technically out with her. He was in the club with his boys and the same bitch I heard in Miami with the squeaky voice was all in his snaps. At one point, she had his phone and was making videos dancing, and he was nowhere to be found. In order for that to happen, Jovaughn must have been fucked up. He never even let me get his phone like that, and we were damn near an unofficial couple. In the past year, we'd gone to Vegas and New York together. Just a week ago, he'd given me money to completely refurnish my apartment. I had added a few more designer bags to my collection and for my birthday, he'd purchased me an iced out Cartier watch. Jovaughn and I had sex at least four times a week. So while I knew there were other women, I knew that I was at the top of the list, so I still didn't nag him or pressure him about being in a relationship with me.

I was spending the night with him and this nigga came in around ten with Hulk's ten-year-old son talking about she had an emergency and Demarco was spending the night with him. I was a little irritated, but I knew he looked at Demarco like a son, so I didn't trip. But when that nigga came from the bedroom dressed to go to the club, I damn near lost it. I shot up off the couch like a rocket.

"You out your mind if you think I'm baby-sitting while you go out to the club," I said in a hushed voice so the kid wouldn't hear me. After all, it wasn't his fault.

"You was gon' be here anyway. I told you when you said you were coming over that I was going out to celebrate my mans coming home from prison, and you said cool. Now it's a problem?"

"Yes it is, because you're baby-sitting right now. Me and that girl don't know each other. You think she want her son here with me?"

Jovaughn kissed his teeth. "You bugging. That lil' nigga like my son and if you can't do me this one solid and watch him for two to three hours, then we can just dead this shit right now. You being real foul and selfish. A nigga just spent ten racks getting new furniture for your crib." He looked at me like he wanted to slap the shit out of me. Because I made it a point not to nag him, Jovaughn and I rarely argued, and I rarely saw him upset. He was always the laughing and joking, in a good mood type of nigga.

I didn't even feel like pointing out to him that whenever he found out he had to watch Demarco he should have canceled his plans. What would he had done if I wasn't there? But I didn't even bother. For one, he was right. Jovaughn wasn't my man, and he'd spent more than twenty thousand dollars on me in the past five months. Aside from the fact that he was fucking other women, I really had no reason to complain about our situation. He spent money and time and the sex was amazing. I bit the bullet and sat back down on the couch.

"Thank you." Jovaughn's facial muscles relaxed and he left out of the apartment.

I felt like a fool when he walked out of that door, but watching his snaps made me feel like an even bigger fool. This was that exciting life that I asked for right? I didn't want boring or mundane, I wanted adventure. I made myself log out and not watch anymore because I was real close to leaving and that would mean leaving a ten-year-old alone in an apartment, and I wasn't even sure if that was legal. I was so mad that tears burned my eyes. I attempted to blink them away as I went into Jovaughn's bedroom and grabbed my overnight bag. As soon as his dumb ass walked in that door, I was leaving. I found something to watch on television and before long, I was dozing off.

I jumped up when I heard Jovaughn coming in the apartment. I grabbed my phone and saw that it was almost five in the morning. I looked at him with disgust all over my face. I could tell the bastard was drunk as hell. "Damn, what you still doing up?"

I stood up. "Fuck you," I spat. "You got me all the way fucked up, but you don't have to worry about me ever again, and I mean that shit."

I brushed past him and he grabbed my arm. "What the fuck you tripping for? Throwing temper tantrums and shit."

I'd never revealed to him that I watched his snaps. No matter what I saw or how mad it made me, I never let him know that I watched them. There was no way that I could explain how I knew about ole girl being all in his phone, so I just snatched away from him and I left. In my car, I slammed the door and erupted into tears. This was what I fucking asked for. I had no one to blame but myself.

* * *

I sat in the waiting room of my doctor's office nervous as shit. It had been two days since I stormed out of Jovaughn's apartment. For the past week, I'd been feeling weird as hell. I couldn't really explain it, but I was having a lot of indigestion, gas, and just overall my stomach felt different. One day I may have cramping, the next day, I'd have gas all day. Sometimes it felt as if I were having hunger pains or something even after I ate, it was just weird. I'd also been feeling tired and having headaches. I took two pregnancy tests. The first one was negative and the second one, I couldn't tell if there was a second line or not. If the second line was there, it was faint as hell to the point that I thought I was imagining it. If I was pregnant, then I'd just have to do what I did when I got pregnant by Ryan. Have an abortion. I didn't care who judged me or looked at me crazy. Jovaughn and I weren't even officially a couple, so I didn't want to be stuck in the house pregnant and miserable while he lived his best life during the summer having fun and fucking bitches. No thanks.

There were two white women in the waiting room with me. One had an infant in a carrier, so I assumed maybe she was there for a six-week check-up or something. The other woman didn't look pregnant, but maybe she was early. Maybe she was just there for a routine check-up. My bored ass had just reached over to grab a magazine when the door opened and in walked Robin. She wasn't alone though. Leonard was behind her. The bitch's belly damn near made it through the door before her. She was pregnant. Heat radiated through my body as we locked eyes. I was the first to look away. I clenched my jaw muscles together as I opened the magazine and was so angry that the words on the page damn near looked blurry. Even though I'd only gotten a glance of her, the bitch was glowing. Pregnancy had her already thick thighs damn near rubbing together, and I was sure her ass had doubled in size. She had some long lemonade braids going to the side and hanging down to her waist. I could see their feet, and Leonard's bitch ass had gone with her to the front desk to sign in.

I turned the page as they found seats across the room. "Bae, I left my water bottle in the car. Can you get it for me?" she asked him, and I damn near threw up hearing her call his ass bae.

"Sure, I'll go get it for you." Leonard stood up and walked back outside. Out of all the doctor's offices in the world, this bitch had to come to this one.

About a month after I got back from Miami with Jovaughn, Leonard posted another picture of him and her on some sort of cruise and said that she'd surprised him for his birthday. It seemed like they were really into each other and at that point I just unfollowed him. Now they were expecting a child together, and if I knew Leonard that meant that he'd already proposed or that he would be soon. Regret had just started kicking my ass when the nurse called me to the back. I was embarrassed and hurt, and I didn't even know why. Leonard had every right to be happy. I didn't want him, so he deserved to find someone that did. I just never expected that someone to be Robin. Maybe the way I craved hood niggas was the same way Leonard craved hood bitches. I tried to turn my hood off when I was with him, but I was still way more street than he'd ever be. I turned him on to a lot of rap music, slang, etc.

"How are you doing today?" the nurse greeted me with a smile and a chipper voice.

Nervousness and anger combined had me feeling light headed, but I forced a fake smile. "I'm good."

After she took my vitals, I explained to her what brought me in, and she told me to pee in a cup before putting me in a room to wait for the doctor. Once I was alone, my thoughts drifted back to Robin and Leonard and her calling him bae. I didn't know why it was bothering me so bad. Probably because Robin was a fuckin' snake. She didn't care about us sharing a cousin and having been cool our entire lives; she swooped in and started fucking with my ex right after we broke up. The bitch didn't even wait a few years. Had I seen her ass in person before she got pregnant, I would've run up on her for sure. There was some still some hood in me, and I wasn't scared of her ass. For a minute after I got back from Miami, Alex and I had a strained relationship. We didn't speak for about three months and then I had to get out of my bag and realize that she wasn't wrong for not wanting to be in the middle of the shit. We got past that and things got back to normal with us.

The doctor came in the room and pulled me from my thoughts. "Hi Natalia, how are you doing today?"

"I'm fine." I once again offered a fake smile as I waited for her to get to the point.

"Okay. You said your last period was three weeks ago. Was it a normal period?"

"Umm yes. Well, I normally bleed for five days, but it lasted for about four. Other than that, it was pretty normal."

"Okay. Since you have on a dress I'm going to let you remove your panties and lie back on the table so I can do a vaginal ultrasound because your urine is telling me that you're pregnant which would explain all the issues going on with your indigestion, gas, cramps, etc. Your organs are shifting and your body is changing to accommodate the baby. No morning sickness?"

My eyebrows furrowed as I took in everything that she was saying. "No. I haven't thrown up or anything. Sometimes when I get indigestion, I feel a little nauseous too, but that's normally just after I eat." I took a deep breath and stood up to remove my panties, then I got back on the table and laid back as she'd asked me to. This wasn't the shit that I needed in my life.

My heart beat a little faster than normal as I waited for the doctor to get everything situated with the machine. Once the instrument was inside me, I winced a tad bit from the pressure on my bladder. It was making me feel like I had to pee. After a few moments of discomfort and silence, the doctor spoke. "There's the fetus right there." She pointed at something white on the screen. "According to the measurements and development, you are ten weeks. The bleeding that you experienced could have been from a number of things, but it wasn't a normal menstrual cycle. If it was shorter than normal and lighter than normal, we wouldn't consider that a regular cycle for you. This little button is developing quite nicely. So according to your last normal cycle, your due date would be December fifteenth."

Due date my ass. I wasn't about to let that happen. Just as soon as I had the thought, the heartbeat filled the room loud and clear. Hearing my child's heartbeat made me feel like scum for being so fast to come to the conclusion that I was getting rid of it. For as much as I liked Jovaughn, hell I think I even loved him, I wasn't naïve enough to think that a baby would change him. It would probably only bring misery to the situation, and I wasn't ready for that. I wasn't even sure how he would feel about having a child with me. We'd never discussed kids, but I knew that he loved Demarco like he was his.

The rest of everything that the doctor said to me was a blur. I also heard her say something about writing me a prescription for prenatal vitamins and making an appointment for my check-up. I didn't even feel that was necessary, but I was going to do it just to avoid having to answer any questions. It was my decision, but I didn't feel like looking a middle-aged white woman with five kids in the face and explaining to her that I was going to terminate the pregnancy. I got dressed slowly, not knowing quite how to feel. As I left the room, I heard that familiar laugh coming from across the hall. Leonard and Robin must have been in the room across the hall. The door was closed, but I heard his loud ass laugh. The doctor must have left my room and gone straight to theirs because I heard her voice.

"Baby girl is doing excellent, and in five weeks, she'll be ready to make her grand entrance. You excited Dad?"

"Man, I can't wait." The excitement in Leonard's voice was impossible to miss. Tears streamed down my face as I put my head down and rushed to the door. I didn't even make another appointment or bother to check out. I just wanted to go home, be alone and cry over the mess that I had made of my life.

# QUASHON

"Shit!" My eyes jerked open as I felt my car scrape something as it veered off the road. A mailbox maybe. I wasn't sure what it was, but I grabbed the steering wheel fast as hell and straightened the car back up.

My cup of lean was sitting between my legs. I'd been sipping on it for hours, and my dumb ass fell asleep while I was on my way home. It was three in the morning, and I had been out hustling all day. I was seventeen and had officially dropped out of high school. Ebony and Tristan lived with me, and she was a senior in high school. She got him up in the morning and took him to daycare before going to school, allowing me to sleep in. I'd then get up around noon and head out to make money. She got out of school at 2:45 and she would come home and study and do her homework before Tristan came home. I picked him up for her at 5:30, took him home, fed him, gave him a bath, and hit the streets again until around one in the morning. Ebony had plenty of help with Tristan as far as me and daycare. She didn't even need her mom or anyone in her family to watch him during the week. She got time to herself while he was in daycare that I paid for, and I still came in, in the evenings and fed and bathed him. No one could any longer call me a deadbeat. I wasn't no king pin or nothing, but I was making around $1,500 a day, sometimes a little more.

Shit, me and Ebony were hood couple goals. After my brother had been dead for about three months, I had enough money to buy her a little Impala that was seven years old, but it ran good as hell. We lived together, and I kept her hair, nails, toes, and all that shit done. Plus, I took care of my son. In my eyes, she had no reason to complain but she did because one, I had started drinking lean bad as hell after my brother died. I drank the shit all day sometimes. Tonight was my second time falling asleep while driving. When I was tired as hell and just couldn't sleep or I didn't have lean, that shit made me cranky as hell. When I got like that, it was like I turned into Quadim reincarnated. I still never put my hands on Ebony though. A few times she got mad and took Tristan and went to her mom's house, but she always came back. I didn't give a fuck what she said. She knew she had it good with me. I made it so she didn't have to go to work. She was a statistic as far as being a teenage mom, but she was about to graduate from high school and go to college. Because I stepped up to the plate and started handling my business, her nor my son wanted for anything, and she wasn't dependent on government assistance.

I'd also gotten caught cheating a few times. Shit, I'm young as hell and the thots be throwing me the pussy. I'm not supposed to take that shit? I'm with Ebony because of my son. She had grown on me though and I did love her, but I wasn't 'bout to be tied down to just one female right now. Fuck all that. She's my girl, and I made other hoes respect her, but I'm gon' do what I do, and that's just the bottom line. My heart was beating fast as hell from swiping that mailbox. I was glad that I was only five minutes from home. Once I pulled up in the driveway, I hopped out of the car and used the flashlight on my cell phone to survey the damage to the car. It wasn't too bad but some of the paint was scratched, and there was a slight dent in the passenger side door. The cheapest I could probably get the shit fixed would be around a thousand dollars. Fuck it. I went into the house, took a shower, ate some food, and passed out.

"Quashon wake yo' bitch ass up!" Something hit me in the back of the head, and I jumped up out of the bed fast as hell. I could barely see, but I knew the voice that was yelling and calling me names was Ebony.

I took a step back as I wiped my eyes. "Fuck wrong with you?" I barked. I didn't even know what time it was, but the sun was shining through the window.

I blinked hard trying to clear my vision, and Ebony hit me in the face and head again with a pillow. I stepped towards her and snatched the pillow from her hands. She was mad as fuck, but I didn't give a damn what she was mad about. She wasn't about to keep hitting me with a fuckin' pillow. "Chill the fuck out!" I tossed the pillow on the bed.

"Nigga why the fuck am I sitting in math class and I get a call from the clinic telling me you gave me an STD? I told you my got damn pussy was burning and you tried to say it was the soap I was using. You nasty, dirty dick ass nigga! Who you been fucking?" She mushed me in the face so hard that my head snapped back far as hell.

"Bitch stop hitting me!" I growled. She'd waken me up out of my sleep with so much bullshit that I could barely process what was going on. Then she wanted to keep hitting on me.

"Bitch?!" she screeched. Ebony was on my ass like white on rice as she hit me in the chest and clawed at my face. I felt like since she wouldn't stop hitting me that she wanted to fight, so I balled my fist up and punched her ass dead in the face. I hit her so hard something cracked, and her nose hurt my damn hand upon the impact. Ebony stopped hitting me and howled in pain as her hands flew up to her nose.

"I told you to stop hitting me," I yelled as my chest heaved up and down. She ran into the bathroom crying. I needed a fucking blunt. Ebony was telling me that I had a damn STD. I had fucked three girls besides her in the last two months, but I only hit one of them raw. That hoe ass Markia.

No sooner than I sparked my blunt, Ebony stormed out of the bathroom with rage in her eyes and specks of blood on her shirt. "You a dumb ass nigga. I think you broke my fuckin' nose. You going to jail bitch," she fussed as she moved around the room and started pulling her clothes from the dresser drawers.

I sat down on the edge of the bed and smoked my blunt as she packed her clothes and talked shit. "No good ass nigga. Yo' nasty ass wanna be out here fucking these dirty butt ass broads, then be having the nerve to come in the house and kiss on my son. Then you put your hands on me," she screeched like she hadn't hit me a gang of times, but I guess that didn't count.

The weed calmed me down, and I was able to tune her out. I thought about the fact that I was going to have to go to the doctor and take medication all because Markia burnt me. I had half a mind to go stick my foot in her ass. "Fuckin' drug addict junkie," Ebony seethed pissing me off.

I shot up off the bed. "You done called me a lot of muhfuckin' names, and I ate that shit 'cus you got a right to be mad, but yo. You being real reckless with your mouth. Talk about how you was stressing going to school and working while taking care of a baby, but because of me you don't have to work. Talk about how I pay for daycare and do shit for my son every day to lighten your load and make it so you can keep your grades up and have time to yourself. Talk about how for your birthday, I paid more than two bands for you to go out and have a good ass time with your ugly ass homegirls," I yelled.

Ebony stopped packing her clothes and looked at me. "What the fuck does that have to do with the fact that you're out here sticking dick in different broads, but you're supposed to be my man? Tell me what that has to do with the fact that you drink lean and smoke weed too got damn much. You're fucking your body up, and you don't even realize it."

I waved her off. "What the fuck ever."

"Yeah, you're not going to be happy until you end up like your dead ass brother."

Hearing her disrespect Quadim like that, did something to me. I swear I didn't mean to, but it's like I had an out of body experience. I flew off the bed and over to her before I could even process what I was doing, and I blacked out. I just knew that after a good sixty seconds, she was on the floor screaming and begging for me to stop. I had just raised my foot to stomp her ass out, when I snapped back to reality. I glared down at her tear streaked face, and it dawned on me just what I was doing. All the times I listened to Quadim and Alex fight, and even though she didn't cry, I used to be on the verge of tears wishing that he'd just leave her alone.

I looked down at my son's mother and realized that I'd just beat the fuck out of her. Even though she'd said some messed up shit, what I'd done wasn't even cool. She got up off the floor still crying, grabbed her keys and left. She didn't even take any of the things that she'd packed. I knew I'd messed up big time. She was going to come back for her stuff, and she was going to take my son away from me. Being a young father, trying to be a good father when I never had one, trying to provide, and trying to forget about the fact that Quadim was dead, it all had me on some other shit. Ebony was right. I needed drugs just to cope with life, so in a sense, I was a junkie. I just wasn't down bad like the fiends I sold heroin to. The ones that would give up their own flesh and blood children for a baggie of some dog food. Nah, I wasn't down bad like that, but I was headed down that road, and the shit made me sad. For as much as I loved him and as much as I missed him, the one person that I never wanted to be like was Quadim. Slowly but surely, I was turning into him.

After Ebony left, I wasn't even sure how long I sat there before my phone rang. Looking at the screen and seeing that it was Markia made my upper lip curl into a snarl. Burning ass bitch. "What?" I barked into the phone. Markia was a senior like Ebony, but she went to a different high school.

"What?" she repeated. "Why you answering the phone with an attitude?"

"'Cus you burning ass bitch. You gave me some shit, and I gave it to my girl." It dawned on me that Ebony hadn't even told me what she had. I guess I would have to go to the doctor and find out for myself, and I wasn't looking forward to it.

There was a slight pause. "I don't know what—"

"Save the shit muhfucka. You can lie to somebody else. Just admit that you a thot. I know my girl ain't fucking nobody else, 'cus when she not in school, she at home with me and our son. She don't even get down like that. You, on the other hand, was sucking on me the second time I ever even seen you. You give that shit up way easy, and I'm dumb as fuck for even sticking dick to you raw. You might as well stop calling my phone, 'cus I'll never fuck with you again."

"Whatever Quashon." She had a nerve to sound hurt. "You're the only person I've been with in the last four months, and I put that on my dead granny. I must have had the shit and just didn't know." I frowned up my face in disgust at the fact that she was saying she'd been walking around for months with an STD and didn't know. Come to think of it, barely a week after I hit her was when Ebony started complaining about her pussy not feeling right. A week after that, she made an appointment at the clinic. "You don't have to fuck with me no more. But I was calling to tell you that I'm pregnant."

## ALEX

My breath caught in my throat as I watched Quashon walk into a sneaker store in the mall. It was my first time seeing him since I ran into him at the hospital that time. When he was more than likely visiting Quadim, and he lied to me about why he was there. Still, I heard Quadim's words echoing through my head saying that Quashon didn't have anything to do with setting me up. I believed him. Quashon just wasn't that type. I wasn't sure if I wanted to say anything to him though. Panama told me that Quashon was mean mugging him one day at the store, and I prayed that life hadn't hardened him enough that he would test Panama's gangsta. He wouldn't win. I would feel funny speaking to him knowing that I killed his brother, but it hurt that after I helped raise him for two years that I could see him and not speaking was even an option. Finally, after some contemplating, I decided to go say hello.

I walked into the store and saw him holding a sneaker in his hand and asking the salesman for his size. I waited patiently until they were done talking. "Hi Quashon." I walked over to him, amazed at how tall he'd gotten since I saw him last.

He turned to face me and his facial muscles relaxed at the sight of my face. "What's going on Alex?" He truly looked happy to see me.

"I can't get a hug?" I asked hopefully.

He walked over and hugged me. "Listen, about that night—"

I cut him off. "I don't want to talk about it. It's over. I'm here, and I'm okay." I offered him a small smile.

Quashon gave a quick head nod. "I have a son now."

My eyes widened with surprise. "Quashon are you serious? You have a son?" He smiled, nodded, and showed me pictures. To my relief, the baby looked very happy and well taken care of. Quadim didn't have the sense of a bed bug, so I prayed that Quashon's baby mama wasn't some lil' hood rat type girl, or that baby wouldn't stand a chance. "He's adorable," I gushed over the chunky baby.

"Thanks."

"You still in school?" I asked, afraid of the answer. I was willing to bet that he wasn't, but I was hoping for more surprises.

"Nah. Just wasn't my thing. Plus, I have a kid to take care of now."

I nodded my head. He'd been doing his own thing for quite a while. Quadim had been dead for a minute, so I wasn't even going to waste my time preaching. I just wished things would have turned out different for Quashon. "Please be careful. I mean it. Quashon, I don't care what me and your brother went through, I will always have love for you. You got that?"

"Did your dude kill my brother?" he asked, catching me off guard. There was a hint of anger in his eyes, and I knew that Panama hadn't been exaggerating about their last encounter. Quashon was definitely at that age where he was doing grown men shit out in the streets.

"Quashon no, he didn't. I wasn't even sure that Quadim was the one that shot me that night. I didn't even know if I was seeing shit because—"

"Because you thought he was dead? He told me Castillo and your dude almost killed him. Look, I don't have nothing to do with that, and I hate the things my brother did to you. At the end of the day, he was still my brother though, and I don't have to like your dude. Bottom line."

"No you don't. You be good out here in these streets and be safe Quashon." I wasn't even about to argue with him about Panama. He had a right not to be buddy buddy with Panama, but if he was thinking of somehow trying to avenge Quadim, then he was barking up the wrong tree.

He no doubt had to mature fast, but he was still a child, and if he knew what was good for him, he'd stay in a child's place. My love for him wouldn't keep Panama off his ass if Quashon violated, and if I had to choose between the two, I was choosing my nigga. Hands down.

* * *

"Are you sure about this?" I asked Natalia. She'd come over and asked me to take her to get an abortion in a few days.

"Yes, I'm sure. Jovaughn and I aren't even on good terms right now. If I wait too much longer, I'll be three months. I just want to get it over with."

"People have arguments all the time. You really want to end your pregnancy because you and him are beefing? What about next week when you two are speaking again?"

Natalia shook her head adamantly. "Jovaughn has more women than I can keep up with. Me having his baby isn't going to stop that. Why should I be stuck in the house with his child while he's out running the streets with different women?"

I shrugged my shoulders. It was her choice. I said my peace, and I was done. If she wanted to keep getting abortions, that was her business. Natalia was a grown woman. Her phone rang, and she kissed her teeth. "We spoke the bastard up. He probably sees my car out here."

The phone continued to ring. "You not gonna answer it?"

"Nope. Fuck him."

I chuckled. Pregnancy hormones had to have Natalia feeling some kind of way because normally, she would jump for Jovaughn's ass. My doorbell rang, and I wondered if it was him. People rarely came by my apartment unexpected. I didn't like a lot of company anyway, but Panama for sure didn't play that shit. When I looked out of the peephole and saw who it was, my eyes bulged out. "Fuck," I mouthed to myself. Robin never came by unexpected, but she wanted to pick this day.

I hoped that she and Natalia would behave because they weren't going to tear up my shit. Robin would buck pregnant or not, but she was too far along, and her belly was too big for them to be acting like asses. Before I could open the door, Natalia came into the room. "Is it Jovaughn?" she asked in a hushed voice. "He keeps calling me."

I shook my head no and opened the door. "Hey, what are you doing here?" I asked Robin in a friendly voice.

She came right on in talking a mile a minute. "I just left the mall and then my bladder started tripping all of a sudden. I have one more stop to make before I go home, and I hate public restrooms. You're right by the Home Goods store I'm on my way to, so I decided to see if you were home." When Robin stopped talking, she realized that I wasn't alone. "Oh, hey Natalia," she stated in a friendly tone.

I didn't even have to turn to look at Natalia to know that her nostrils were probably flaring. I wouldn't have been surprised if smoke came out of her ears. "You have a lot of fuckin' nerve to speak to me after you fucked my nigga. You didn't speak to me when you saw me at the doctor. Don't be fake now bitch."

Oh shit. I took a deep breath. To my surprise, Robin smiled. "I didn't speak then because you looked uncomfortable. I'm not fake, I was being cordial. You don't have to speak to me, it's no big deal, but watch that bitch word. I don't like it."

"Bitch fuck you!" Natalia's voice rose an octave. "Like I said, you're fake as fuck. We used to see each other every summer. You've spent the night at my house before when we were kids. We're not related, but we share family. Now you're pregnant by my ex, and I'm supposed to be cool with you? You smoking dick bitch."

"Yeah we share family, and we were cool when we were kids. I've never even been in the same room with you and Leonard as an adult. It may have been wrong, but men like him don't come around that often. I wasn't about to pass up a good man just because you didn't know what to do with him. I've never been happier in my life, so nah, I don't feel bad worth a damn. I'm glad you fucked him over."

"I bet you are! Leonard isn't even your type. You're using him and his ass is too stupid to see it. That's why I was there too because he's a good man and a provider. Eventually though, you're going to want to go back to what you know. Hood ass niggas," Natalia spat.

Robin chuckled and rubbed her protruding belly in a circular motion. "You childish as fuck. How do you know what my type is? Baby, I'm a grown woman. My type is a stable man, with good credit, a bank account, career, 401k, and treats me well. That's my type. I used hood niggas to my advantage, but don't you ever say I'm using Leonard if you don't know what the fuck you're talking about. I've used plenty niggas and never got pregnant by one or married. Yeah bitch." Robin held up her hand to display the huge rock on her finger. "Me and Leonard got married last week, and $5,000 of the down payment on our new home came from *my* bank account. The furniture for our bedroom and the living room was purchased with *my* credit card. I don't have to use Leonard for his money. I'm not a broke, needy bitch like you were."

"Okay y'all, I think—" Before I could attempt to defuse the situation, Natalia was walking towards Robin, and I jumped in front of her. "Both y'all are pregnant, and you don't need to be fighting," I shouted just as Robin stepped to the side, reached around me and grabbed Natalia by the hair.

I got pissed the fuck off when I was accidentally hit in the mouth while trying to break the shit up. I was ready to slap fire out of both their stupid asses. They were disrespecting my apartment, fighting while pregnant, and the whole scene was a shit show. I moved my ass right out of the way and let the dummies fight. Robin was getting the best of Natalia, big belly and all. My front door opened, and Panama walked in and looked over at me with wide eyes.

"Yooo what the fuck?" he barked loud as hell. "Y'all got to get the fuck outta here with that bullshit," he snapped, pissed the fuck off.

Surprisingly, they stopped fighting. Both of them were out of breath, breathing hard, chests heaving up and down. Panama had a deep scowl on his face, and his eyes darted back and forth between the two of them. Natalia snatched her purse and keys up off the couch. "Fuck you, fuck Leonard, and fuck that bastard ass baby."

Robin made a move towards Natalia, and Panama stopped her. "Chill out," he stated through clenched teeth as Natalia slammed our front door. His head whipped in my direction. "Yo Alex, I'm mad close ma," he warned.

I knew he'd be pissed at our home being disrespected. Shit, I was pissed too, especially about my lip.

"Ahhhhhhh," Robin let out a deep groan as she doubled over in pain.

I instantly forgot all about being angry and rushed over to her. "What's wrong?"

She grabbed her stomach with one hand and the wall with the other. "Contraction," she managed to pant. "Fuckkkk, it hurts so bad. I still have four weeks before she's due."

"I'm calling an ambulance," I stated, looking around for my phone as Panama led her over to the couch. The day was going from bad to worse and to think, I'd been home in the kitchen minding my business, cooking before all of this went down.

The contraction subsided as I spoke with the 9-1-1 dispatcher, and Robin got up to go in the bathroom. The dispatcher assured me that she was on the way, and I ended the call. "Fuck happened?" Panama asked me.

I shook my head back and forth. "Robin popped up over here to use the bathroom while Natalia was here, and shit went left real quick. I tried to break them up and got hit in the mouth. Robin knows she's too far along to be fighting like she's crazy. I have a fucking migraine." Just as I leaned against the wall, Robin let out a gut wrenching howl, and I darted down the hall to the bathroom.

She opened the bathroom door, doubled over in pain, with a tear streaked face and blood soaking the seat of her sweatpants.

# PANAMA

"What a fucking day," I stated as Alex and I lay cuddled up in the bed. Her head was on my chest, and my arms were wrapped around her. We'd just spent five hours at the hospital with Robin and Leonard. She was good, she just lost her mucus plug, or whatever you call that shit, right after the fight, and the blood made her freak out.

Her baby was born four weeks early, but she weighed five pounds, and the doctors felt like she was going to be fine. She was breathing a little fast, so they put her in the NICU. Alex sighed. "Tell me about it. I will never, ever let both of them anywhere near me at the same time again. For as fucked up as Natalia is, she has a small point. Her and Robin go back to childhood. They're cool through me, but still, they had enough of a friendship that Leonard should have been off limits to Robin. However, Leonard is a good guy, and he deserves to be happy. Natalia kept shitting on him, and he got her ass back. They just need to get over it."

I ran my fingers through Alex's hair. "That's that female drama, but I feel Leonard though. 'Cus if you did me dirty how she did him dirty, you might walk in and catch me fuckin' ya moms." Alex lifted her head and looked at me.

"Really nigga?"

"You damn right. Hopefully, Robin is going to be too busy with a baby to entertain the dumb shit, and Natalia just needs to find her some business."

"Agreed."

"You know what I've been thinking about?" I asked Alex thoughtfully.

"What?"

"Going to the courthouse and just getting married. Like in a year or two when you're almost done with school and we're settled in our house, and my businesses are booming, we can have a big ass wedding. It's not about that though. It's just about us rocking the same last name. None of the extra shit matters."

Alex sat up again but that time, she had an excited gleam in her eyes. "Are you serious Panama? You really want to get married?"

"Why not? We can apply for the license tomorrow. Then just give it a few days to find you the perfect ring, and we can be married by next weekend."

"I don't even need a ring right now. We can get married tomorrow, and I wouldn't care about the ring. We can get matching tattoos. Like you said, none of the extra shit matters. A ring will let niggas know that I'm off the market, but you don't have to spend all this money on a ring to make me happy. You make me happy." I could tell by the look in her eyes, she meant that shit.

"Word? You gone make the kid blush and shit," I joked as she straddled me then proceeded to place soft kisses along my chest. She moved down slowly, pulled my dick from my boxer briefs and began to suck slowly at first, then she increased the pace. "Damn baby," I moaned as she gagged a little when my dick hit her tonsils, but she didn't break the rhythm.

All the shit I had endured since coming home, all of it was worth it to get to the end result which was Alex becoming my wife. That little beef with Quadim was light work. None of the drama that he brought was enough to keep me away from Alex.

"Yooooo," I breathed as she relaxed her jaws and throat and it felt as if my dick was damn near down her shit. "Fuck Alex," I panted as my toes curled.

She sucked all the spit off my dick, then eased down on it. She didn't wear panties to bed so she had none to remove. I held onto her ass with both hands as she rode my dick while staring into my eyes.

"So my by the end of the day tomorrow you're going to have my last name?" I asked her.

Alex nodded as she leaned down onto my chest and covered my lips with hers. She snaked her tongue into my mouth and came all on my dick. Between the sloppy ass head that she gave me and the death grip her juicy pussy had on my dick, I came with her, and that shit had never happened. We'd only been fucking for about five minutes. Only time I ever came that fast was when I got pussy for the first time and the first pussy that I got when I was released from prison. I wasn't even embarrassed though because my dick was still hard, so I flipped her over onto her back and murdered the pussy. I had the rest of our lives to make up for that quick nut.

* * *

"I can't believe you got married nigga. Ma is mad as hell that you didn't tell her," Butta shouted into my ear over the loud music in the club.

"I keep trying to tell you and her that it was some last minute shit. The only other person there was her friend Jessica as the witness. Her family wasn't there. Plus, she's going to plan a big ass wedding. We're just not doing it until she finishes nursing school. Look," I held my hand out revealing the tattoo of a K for king on my ring finger. "We haven't even been shopping for rings. That's how last minute it was."

"Y'all niggas got married and didn't exchange rings. I know the Justice of the Peace thinks y'all some broke pieces of shit." Butta laughed, and I laughed too.

"Fuck what that nigga thinks. Me and Alex know what it is. Plus, we got married in matching red bottoms, and she had some iced out studs in her ear. The last thing we looked was broke. Believe that shit."

"I'm happy for you my G. For real. Who would have thought that you'd get married before me?"

"I know right, but check this. Alex's dad is going to get the pounds from me. He understands my situation, and he's trying to make some extra money on the side. He says that being that he's in Miami, if the weed is any good, he can tax white boys, tourists, celebrities, and all that good jazz. He's willing to pay me $400 more per pound than what I paid, so I won't take a complete loss."

"That's what's up. So you out for good?"

"I guess." I sighed regretfully. "I wanted to make a little bit more money but being greedy can be a nigga's downfall. I'm a husband now, so I gotta do what I gotta do to make sure I can stay out here on these streets. Me and my shorty just gonna work hard and travel until she's ready to give me some babies."

"That's what it is then." Butta gave me dap, and I finished off my beer.

As I looked at my watch, I saw that the club closed in thirty more minutes. "I'm 'bout to be out. You ready?"

"Yeah."

"That's the nigga that killed my brother," I heard a voice say the moment I stepped outside of the club.

"I thought your brother died from a drug overdose."

"Nah. Quadim didn't shoot no fuckin' heroin. Anybody that knew my brother knew that shit."

I had a gun in my car, but I didn't even need to get to the gun. Lil' man was trying me, and it was time for me to do something about it. I didn't have to turn around to know who was speaking. I wasn't sure if he had a gun or not, but I didn't give a fuck. I whirled around and saw Quashon and some other lil' dude leaning up against the side of the building. I headed in their direction.

"Yo' lil' nigga, you got some shit you need to say to me?" I asked.

Quashon stood upright and puffed out his chest. "Nigga I said what I said. I think you killed my brother. I'm supposed to be scared of you?"

I wasn't with all the talking. This boy was accusing me of murder, and he obviously felt some type of way about me. If I told him I didn't kill Quadim, he wouldn't believe me, and I would never throw my wife under the bus. If he needed to think that I killed Quadim, then that's what it was. I wasn't about to cop no pleas. I was sick of his mouth and his lil' fucked up looks though. He wanted to be grown, I was gon' handle him like he was grown. I drew my fist back and hit him so hard that he flew back into the building.

His friend took a step towards me, but Butta was on his ass. "Don't even think about it my man."

I hit Quashon with blow after blow for a good minute until he slid down the side of the building. He was dazed and confused as blood trickled down his nose, but I still bent down and got in front of his face. "Ya lil' police ass can stop accusing me of murder all out in public and shit, 'cus I didn't do that nigga. Now, I'm gon' let you live, but next time you even breathe in my direction, it's over for you. It's cute that you trying to ride for your brother and all, but this ain't what you want G." I walked off and left the nigga on the ground.

# QUASHON

After Panama beat my ass, it took me a good five minutes to get up off the ground. It wasn't just the beating though. I'd been drinking lean all day per usual and that shit had me slow as fuck. I should have known better than to start some shit while I had that much lean in my system. Getting beat up in front of anyone was embarrassing as fuck, and I left the club with murder on my mind. I was so pissed off that I left the club speeding, running red lights and all, until my dumb ass got pulled over by the police. I had weed on me, heroin, and a gun, so I got carted right off to jail.

By the time I got my first call, it was almost five in the morning, and I prayed that Ebony would answer the phone. She was back at my house after staying gone for four days. She was still acting mad and not saying much to me, but her mom had a boyfriend, and she was acting like she didn't want Ebony and the baby there. Ebony reluctantly came back to my crib. I knew once she found out that I was supposed to have another baby on the way, that she would flip once again. At the moment, that was the least of my problems though. I was pissed as hell that it was damn near nine pm before I got released. I walked out of the magistrate's office with a frown on my face.

"Got damn. I called you four hours ago. You just now getting to me?" I barked at Ebony.

She looked at me like she wanted to slap the shit out of me. "Nigga you better be glad I came at all! I should have let Markia come get your ass. I wasn't about to wake my baby up and bring him out at no five in the morning to get yo' ass. You got me fucked up."

"Man, now I see why Quadim used to slap bitches," I grumbled as I walked down the steps of the building. I was hungry, and I needed food and a shower. My car got impounded, and Ebony bitched the whole way home. I wanted to just push her ass out of a moving car.

On top of the legal problems that I now had, the fact that Panama whooped my ass in front of my homies was weighing heavily on my mind. I could always catch him slipping and run up on him with a gun, but I was just gon' leave it alone. I knew Quadim wasn't a saint, and I was still running around trying to ignite beef on his behalf. Lesson learned. Now because of it, I'd caught a bullshit ass charge, and by the time my final court date rolled around, I'd probably be eighteen so I couldn't play the juvenile card. I was aggravated to the tenth power.

Ebony whipped the car up in the driveway like I gave a damn about her having an attitude. It was taking everything in me not to knock the shit out of her. Police had taken my money, they took drugs, and my gun. Not to mention, I had to give the bail bondsman a little over ten thousand to get me out of jail. That shit put a serious dent in my stash, and I wasn't happy about it. After I took a shower, I was going to get back out on the block and attempt to make some of my money back. When I was in the shower, I started feeling funny as hell. It was almost like I was drunk. I swayed to the left a lil' bit, and I had to lean up against the shower wall to steady myself. Something was off, and I didn't know any other way to describe it. I turned the water off, and attempted to get out of the shower, and I don't remember shit else after that.

* * *

I woke up in the hospital confused as fuck. As soon as I opened my eyes, Ebony jumped up out of the chair that she was sitting in. "Thank God. Quashon you've been asleep for more than ten hours. I thought you weren't ever going to wake up." All the attitude that Ebony had been holding onto for the past few days was gone. She actually looked worried about me and sounded concerned.

"Fuck am I doing in the hospital?" I asked, looking around the room.

"You have a knot on the back of your head, but I don't think it's from when you fell in the shower. You were on your side when I found you. Have you hit your head Quashon?"

"Yeah, last night. I got into a fight at the club. What that gotta do with anything?"

"Quashon who in the world were you fighting?"

"The reason I'm here Ebony?" I wanted her to cut to the chase.

She kissed her teeth, annoyed that I didn't answer her question. "The doctor thinks the fact that you hit your head hard along with the fact that you're detoxing from promethazine, caused you to have a seizure. Quashon, I told you that shit was messing your body up. Going more than a few hours without it caused you to have a seizure. That's not good. First you go to jail and now this. What are you out here doing?"

I lay my head back on the pillow and looked up at the ceiling. I didn't even have an answer to that question.

# NATALIA

"Hello?" the female on the other end of the phone threw me for a loop. For as long as I'd dealt with Jovaughn, no other woman had ever answered his phone before. Just when I'd gathered the nerve to finally return his calls and let him know that in the morning, I'd be getting an abortion, this shit happened.

I had half a mind to hang up the phone, but I didn't. I wanted to curse his ass out one final time and then be done with him. "May I speak to Jovaughn?" I tried not to have an attitude, but I damn sure wasn't about to be sounding all timid and scared. This man had been sticking dick to me for over a year. Fuck whoever was on the other side of the phone.

"Who is this?" The tone of her voice wasn't confrontational, but all of the questions were starting to piss me off. Still, I made an effort to remain calm.

"It's Natalia. He's called me several times over the past few days, and I'm returning his calls." My voice was firm.

"This is Jovaughn's sister. Maybe you should've answered those calls because my brother was killed this morning. They found him in the front yard at some female's house. He'd been robbed and shot in the head. I always told him a bitch would be his downfall." Her voice cracked, and she began to cry before ending the call.

I instantly felt the urge to throw up. "Nooooo," I moaned in a barely audible voice. "Noooooooooo." My voice got just a tad bit louder. This couldn't be right. This had to be a lie. Her words echoed in my head, and I let out a blood curdling scream. I had ignored him for three days. Jovaughn called me more than four times, and I was too mad at him to respond, and now I would never talk to him again.

I cried until I gagged, and that caused me to throw up. Once I'd emptied the contents of my stomach, I gripped the sides of the toilet until my knuckles damn near turned white. Why was this happening? Why? Jovaughn had a lot of women, but he wasn't a bad guy at all. He was always smiling just thinking he was the smoothest nigga in the room. He didn't fucking deserve to die. Why couldn't they have just robbed him and left him alive? The shit wasn't fair. Screaming wasn't even enough; I wanted to punch the fucking wall. I wanted to kick something, knock everything over. I lost track of time. I don't know how long I stayed on my knees gripping the toilet, but eventually I got up.

It didn't matter how many times Alex and I got into arguments or what we argued about, when I was going through something, she was always the first person that I called. And she came every time. I was sitting on the couch with a tear streaked face when she rang the doorbell. Not even thirty minutes after I called her, she was there. As soon as I opened the door, I collapsed into her arms, and she held me as I cried like a baby. I was exhausted, my head hurt, and my throat burned, but as long as my body would produce them, I would shed tears for Jovaughn. It wouldn't bring him back, but I was going to release them. I felt guilty. The words his sister spoke to me sent chills down my spine every time I thought about them. Guilt would forever eat at my soul for not answering the phone for him when he was calling me and for letting him die without knowing that I was carrying his child. Those were two things that I'd never forgive myself for. Ever.

## QUASHON'S EPILOGUE

"Damn, it seem like he got bigger since the last time I seen him." I grinned as Ebony passed my son to me. I got my court case continued for a full year, and then I finally took a plea for nineteen months. I had been locked up so far for ten months. Half my time was done. I couldn't wait to get out of prison and get back to my son and Ebony.

Ebony was in college to be a teacher, and with the money that I left her, she was doing okay. She made it last by applying for food stamps and using her financial aid checks to help out. She wasn't balling, but she was maintaining, and she only worked part-time on the weekends. Markia ended up having a little girl. She brought her to see me twice, but she got mad and stopped coming when I asked for a blood test. Markia was a shade darker than me, and I had a bronzed skin tone. Her daughter was red as hell. I didn't think she was mine, but I wouldn't flat out deny her until a test told me she wasn't mine.

"He is bigger. I swear he's outgrowing his clothes every three months." Ebony shook her head and smiled at Tristan.

"How much money you got left?" I didn't need her to be out there struggling and stressing while I did my bid. The shit would make me feel bad.

"I'm good. I have enough to pay the rent for another four months. By the time that runs out, I'll have gotten my school check, and I can ask for more hours at work when my classes end for summer break. We'll be good Quashon."

A lot had changed since I left the hospital from having that seizure. I wouldn't front like the shit wasn't hard, but I stopped drinking lean. I tried to be a better boyfriend to Ebony, and I spent a lot of my free time hustling and stacking money so my son would be good while I was away. I even told her about Markia's baby, and the fact that she didn't leave me made me appreciate her ass even more. I was lowkey worried that she would leave my ass while I was down, but Ebony was a good girl. Still, even good girls got lonely. There was nothing I could really do about it though.

"I started my GED classes," I informed her.

"That's what's up. I'm proud of you Quashon. You think you'll be able to find a job when you get home? Maybe get your CDL's and drive trucks." There was a hopeful gleam in her eyes. I knew she didn't want me to go back to hustling.

I wasn't going to make her any promises because I would go back to hustling before I allowed myself to be broke, but I was going to make an effort to get a job. "Hopefully I will get a job Eb."

Even though I was in prison, I had come a long way. Even when we went through bullshit, I was thankful for Ebony. Because of her, I wasn't completely alone when Quadim died, and I would forever hold her in my heart for that. Looking at where I came from and how I grew up, even if nobody else was, I was damn proud of myself, and hopefully life would only get better.

## NATALIA'S EPILOGUE

"Oh my god Natalia. Every time I see this baby, she looks more and more like Jovaughn." Alex picked Jarai up and snuggled her close to her chest.

I smiled because she was telling the truth. "I know right. She's his twin." I sat down on the couch and watched my cousin stare down at my three-month-old daughter. After Jovaughn died, I was so depressed that I didn't get out of bed for four days. By the time I did get out of bed, I had missed my appointment to get an abortion, and I didn't have the heart to make another one.

Out of all the time that Jovaughn and I messed around, I had never met anyone in his family. The money, the jewelry, nothing that he had, I had claim to, and I didn't even want anything. He was never technically my man, but I loved him, and I would forever hold our memories dear. All the pictures I had in my phone from our trips, I printed them out and had them enlarged. One was on my living room wall and two were in Jarai's room. I had no intentions on reaching out to any of Jovaughn's family, but someone saw something that I posted on Facebook, and his sister reached out to me. She and her mom visited Jarai a few times and brought her clothes and stuff, but I mostly did everything on my own.

Once I got out of my funk, which lasted about two weeks, I went hard working. I worked myself to death just to stay busy and try to keep from thinking about him. When I wasn't working, I would cry. Work and sleep was how I kept myself occupied for months. By the time my baby was born, she had everything that she needed, and money wasn't something I was stressing. I even worked from home sometimes making extra money helping Alex with her skincare products. She was doing the damn thing, sometimes making more than $10,000 in a month. She and Panama lived in a nice ass house and he worked for his friend Jay. They must have been seeing some good ass money because for her birthday, Panama bought her a Bentley truck.

I wasn't dating, I wasn't interested in dating. I was fine with being alone for a while. My fetish for the fast life and rough men died with Jovaughn. I just wanted to keep working on myself and raise my daughter. I wanted her to be everything that my mother and I weren't. My mom and I were actually getting along better these days. I don't know what miracle occurred, but she was actually being nicer and less harsh and opinionated. She even volunteered to watch Jarai for me a few times because she said I looked tired and needed to rest. I thought of Jovaughn every day, and I loved him and missed him, but I was slowly getting back to normal. It just didn't seem fair that he never got to meet his only child.

"You looking real comfortable over there with my baby. Now Panama done bought you a Bentley truck. When you gon' give that man a baby?"

Alex laughed. "The wedding is in thirty days, so I'm going to stop taking my birth control pills after the honeymoon. I will be pissed off if my period is on the seven days we're in Dubai. Once we get back, I will give him all the babies he wants."

Alex was happy and glowing, and I was so happy that she got away from Quadim with her life. Panama was everything to her. He was that rare thug that was faithful, respectful, and worshipped the ground she walked on. Even though he went to prison during their first relationship, she still seemed to have snagged the perfect thug.

## PANAMA'S EPILOGUE

"What you looking at so hard?" Alex asked as she flopped down on the couch.

I tore my eyes away from my phone to look over at her. "Jay just put me up on some condos he's about to invest in. I think I'm going to do the same thing," I stated excitedly. I had to thank God for putting Jay in my life because that nigga stayed turning me on to investments and legal money. I was trying to be a millionaire before I hit thirty-five on some real shit. Last year, I averaged $200,000 without drug money, and I was trying to double that shit. Castillo was home from prison, and he told me to holla at him if I needed anything, but I was good on that. My girl was a few months away from being an LPN. She already had a job offer making $30 an hour. I didn't need to be risking my freedom. I was good.

"Damn bae, that's what's up."

I put my phone down and pulled her into my lap. "When you gon' get off that birth control though and give a nigga some babies? Got damn."

"Why is this the second time I've been asked that today? After the wedding babe. My birth control pills are going in the trash, and you can shoot my club up day and night until I get pregnant," she giggled.

I smacked her on the ass and kissed her on the lips. "That's what the fuck I'm talking about. All a nigga want is to come home after a long day at work to my wife and some babies."

"You can get that," Alex promised as she gazed into my eyes.

When I walked up out of prison, I wasn't mad at Alex, but I never saw us getting back together, ever. I just felt that I was going to move on and start fresh, but God had other plans. Allowing Alex back into my life and not holding what she did against her was the best thing that I ever did in my life.

The end!

Thank you guys of course for reading this two-part series. I'm not sure if you know, but I also create journals. I have a journal called *Beautiful Me* and I will be picking one reader to send a journal to. All you have to do is show me proof that you left a review. It doesn't have to be a five-star review; I ask for HONEST reviews. I am using this as a way to ensure that one of the winners is someone that supports me. That is why there is criteria concerning a review. If you're not friends with me on social media, you can inbox me or my publisher Porscha Sterling with a screenshot of the review.

Also, you know I'm always working and I love giving you guys sneak peeks of what I have next. I don't have a for sure release date, but check out what's next from me coming in July and titled: *Azaan and Jayda: Lovin' a Haitian Hitta*.

# AZAAN'S EPILOGUE

"Bae, you just gon' stare at me the entire time?" I asked my girl Vickie as I stuffed clothes into my black and grey checkered Louis Vuitton duffel bag. I already had one suitcase full of clothes and personal items. I didn't want to take more than two pieces of luggage, so I was trying to stuff my duffel bag to capacity. I had so much shit, it was hard trying to determine what to take and what to leave behind. I looked over at Vickie, who had been pouting for the past hour.

Her bottom lip was literally sticking out, and she had her arms folded underneath her breasts like an unhappy child. I chuckled, and that made her kiss her teeth. "It's not funny Azaan. You're leaving me and your son here to go to North Carolina where you're telling me you'll be for at least eight months. Why you have to be there for so long, and why can't Aheem and I go?" Her voice cracked, and I knew the tears were about to start.

I zipped my bag while letting out a breath through my nostrils. Vickie knew one thing I lacked was patience, and one of my pet peeves was repeating myself, but I was going to remain calm. "Just like I told you the last two times, I don't shit where I eat. I'm going to unknown territory to set up shop in a city that I know nothing about. Fahan caught his charge in Charlotte, and when he's released from prison, he has to be there on papers for at least a year before he comes back to Miami. I'm going to set shit up for him so when he comes home, he's good. I'm not taking you and my son to a place that I don't know shit about and where I plan on doing hella dirt for the next few months. It's not happening so stop asking." I tossed her a look to let her know that I meant what the hell I said.

The room was silent for a moment as Vickie processed what I'd just said to her. I damn near felt bad for barking on her because she just wanted me close. After all, I was her nigga, so there wasn't anything wrong with that. I was going to miss her and my son, but as her man and his father, their safety came first. I had to feel them North Carolina cats out before I took my family there, and there was nothing she could say to make me change my mind about that. I looked at the platinum Rolex that was secured around my wrist and saw that I had two and a half hours before my plane departed. I walked over to her and stood in front of her.

I took in the chocolate hue of Vickie's skin. I raised my hand and caressed her chin as I peered into her cat-shaped eyes. My dick grew in my jeans as I eyed her luscious D cup breasts. I removed my hand from her chin and untied the belt on her green silk robe. I bit my bottom lip as I took in her dark skin in the peach bra and panty set she was wearing. "Take this shit off," I demanded in a low voice.

Vickie stood up and did as I asked. She removed her robe, then her bra. The moment her panties hit our beige carpeted floor, I was rubbing on her ass and tonguing her down. She unbuckled my belt, and I broke the kiss. "You know a nigga gon' miss you. You also know how I feel about my family. No way I'm letting my brother come home to nothing. I'm gon' set shit up, and then I'll be back in two weeks to visit. Stop that pouting shit and be the woman that I need you to be." My voice was low but firm.

Vickie nodded her head, and I grabbed a handful of her hair as I devoured her lips again. She liked that rough shit, and I did too. I whirled her around and placed my hand in the center of her back. Pushing her down, I dropped my jeans and boxer briefs and stuffed dick all in her pink slit. "Babbyyy," she cried out as she gripped a handful of our white comforter.

I watched her ass jiggle as I gripped her waist and pounded in and out of her. Time was of the essence, so I needed to make sure that we both got ours in as little time as possible. Reaching around her, I used my pointer finger to stroke her clit, and Vickie threw her head back. I loved it when she didn't wear weave, 'cus that meant I could yank her shit hard as hell without worrying about it coming off. I hated them lacefront joints. I'd rather she do the sew-in, but I guess that wasn't "popping" no more.

I grabbed her thick curls and pounded into her harder. "Cum on this dick," I demanded, and she let out an erotic moan.

With a firm grip still on her hair, I leaned down and began sucking on her neck, and her pussy began spraying like an oozie. "That's what the fuck I'm talkin' 'bout," I growled as she came.

Once she was done, I pulled out of her. "Eat this shit up," I panted and watched her get on her knees and take me into her mouth. She cleaned all of her honey off my dick, and then deep throated me until I was shooting my seeds down her throat.

My legs were weak as fuck as I walked to the bathroom to clean up, but I didn't have time to waste. "Get dressed so you can run me to the airport," I called out as I turned the water on at our his and hers sinks and grabbed a washcloth. It's just me, Vickie, and our two-year-old son at the crib, but we lived in a five-bedroom, four-bathroom house in a gated community.

My father was in Haiti, and my mother died four years ago from breast cancer. My aunt Joie and my brother Fahan were all the family that I had in the states. I'm the oldest, so when my mother died, I was the beneficiary on her life insurance policy. When she died, I was twenty years old, making petty money, committing petty crimes. Stealing cars, robbing niggas. Just living fast, reckless, and dangerous. I took the $35,000 that was left after the funeral and got my own place, a piece of shit car, and I invested the rest in molly, meth, and ecstasy. In the four years since then, I'd more than quadrupled that investment.

When my mom died, Fahan was nineteen. He was in college playing ball and getting decent grades, but when she died something in him changed. The nigga transferred to NC State and was only there a few months before he'd dropped out of school and started selling weed. A year after that, he caught a charge, and he'd been locked up for the past year with six more to go. I was going to Charlotte to make sure when he came home, he didn't come home wanting for shit. I was pretty much doing the damn thing in Miami, but that wasn't enough. It was time to expand and get some of that good old North Carolina money.

Aheem was with Vickie's mom, so she got dressed in a one-piece denim catsuit and red YSL heels. She slicked her hair back in a ponytail and grabbed the keys to my Wraith. I was going to let her flex and drive the shit while I was gone. For the moment, I was going to fly to North Carolina and get a rental car to get around in. When I came back in two weeks, I was either going to drive the Wraith back or my BMW truck. I hadn't decided yet. I had three cars and Vickie had two.

"I signed Aheem up for swim classes. I'm also going to teach yoga two days a week at the Y, and I'll probably help Mommy at the store. I'm going to be pretty busy while you're gone."

I looked over at her. She was acting like a big girl, and I appreciated that. "That's what's up. You stay busy, and the time will fly by. You know I never stay away too long." I placed my head on the headrest.

"Yeah, just don't be in North Carolina on no other shit Azaan. I know why you're going, but I also know that I won't be there while plenty of other bitches will. Temptation is a muhfucka," she stated with a hint of warning in her tone. "We been doing good. Let's keep it like that."

I let out a light chuckle. "Yes ma'am." Vickie and I had been together for four years. I met her a month after my mom died, and on one hand I needed someone in my life to comfort me and cater to me, but on the other hand, some days my grief got the best of me and I was an asshole.

Despite my up and down moods, Vickie was patient with me, and she didn't get tired of my shit right away. She tried to hold me down, but once I started really wildin' and she caught me with a female one night, that's when she finally left me alone. We didn't speak for five months, and I ended up seeing her one day, and she had a big belly. She told me the child she was carrying was mine, but I didn't believe it. I had started making a little money, so I figured if she was knocked up by me, she wouldn't hesitate to tell me and try to use it to her advantage, but I was wrong. When Aheem was born, we had a blood test done, and he ended up being mine. From there, I moved her in with me, and we became a family. When I'm out of town in Puerto Rico, Hawaii, Vegas, or anywhere else, and I have the chance to fuck a bad bitch, I do. Sue me. It is what it is, but I'm not just running around here playing Vickie crazy. I actually hadn't even cheated on her in a long ass time. At least eight or nine months. I was still young, but I'd been living fast since the age of seventeen. I was content with chasing money and then going in the house where it was safe.

My son was only two, and I took pride in the fact that most of the shit he knew, I taught him, and that came from spending time. I had him reading words like red, two, and cup, off flashcards. He was already potty trained, and he could count to ten. I did that shit. Not a tutor, not Vickie, but me. I couldn't wait to teach him about sports, how to fish, all that shit.

Vickie and I made small talk all the way to the airport, and once I arrived, she put the car in park, got out and walked around to hug me. "I love you. Please be safe."

I gave her a quick peck on the lips. "You already know. I love you too." After giving her a quick smack on the ass, I grabbed my luggage from the trunk of the car and headed inside the airport.

Bars, nightclubs, strip clubs, all that shit was cliché for drug dealers to own, but in my case, it made good ass sense. Two days earlier, I'd sent my homie Nas to Charlotte with meth, ecstasy, molly, and Xanax pills. The ecstasy and molly were party drugs for sure, and it made good sense to open up a strip club where dancers and customers could indulge. In Miami, some of everybody fucked with everything, but I knew in Charlotte, the majority of my meth customers would more than likely be white. For them and the people that wanted to get pills outside of club hours, I had a lil' spot in the hood. My brother's homie Pookie had hipped me and Nas to certain areas, turned us on to a few users to get the ball rolling, and all that good shit.

Vickie and I came down the month before and the building for the strip club, the liquor permit, etc., were all in her name. In all honesty, she and my son could have come to Charlotte with me, but I really did like keeping my family and business separate. Plus, it would give me a chance to breathe just a little bit. I didn't really have plans to do anything, but without Vickie there waiting for me, I could come in when I wanted and just do what I wanted without hearing anybody's mouth. I was about to be keeping a lot of crazy hours, shit was going to be stressful, and I didn't need a nagging ass female in my ear. I just hoped Fahan's ass would come home and appreciate everything that I was doing for him.

## ABOUT THE AUTHOR

Natisha Raynor discovered her love for reading in third grade. As she got older she preferred being in her bedroom reading a good book versus playing outside. Natisha began writing her own stories at 12 years old, when the books she was reading no longer held her interest. Natisha wrote for fun for many years until she reached her mid-twenties and sought out a publishing deal. In 2015 she self-published her first novel and since then she's penned more than thirty books. Natisha resides in Raleigh, North Carolina with her two teenaged children.

***Stay Connected:***
If you haven't already joined my reading group, please do so: My Heart Beats Books

facebook.com/Natisha-Raynor-Presents-1003152116362757
instagram.com/author_natisha_raynor

## ALSO BY NATISHA RAYNOR

Idris and Wisdom: The Most Savage Summer Ever (3 book series)

Cherished by a Thug (2-Book series)

In Love with the King of North Carolina (3 book series)

Shawty got a Thang for them Country Boys (3 book series)

Married to a Haitian Mob Boss (2 book series)

A Gangsta and His Shawty: Heirs to the Baptiste Throne (2 book series)

For the Love of You

In Love with the Hood in Him (2 book series)

Aashiem and Hysia: A Dope Boy Love Story

A'san and Bishop: A Thug's Obsession

When Love is Stronger than Pride

Torn Between A Boss And A Real One (2 book series)

She's Got A Thug In His Feelings (2 book series)

Fallin' For A Carolina Menace (2 book series)

Southern Thugs Do It Better (3 book series)

She Made A Savage Change His Ways

For my full catalog check out my

Amazon Author Page

**Royalty Publishing House** is now accepting manuscripts from aspiring or experienced urban romance authors!

## WHAT MAY PLACE YOU ABOVE THE REST:

Heroes who are the ultimate book bae: strong-willed, maybe a little rough around the edges but willing to risk it all for the woman he loves.

Heroines who are the ultimate match: the girl next door type, not perfect - has her faults but is still a decent person. One who is willing to risk it all for the man she loves.

The rest is up to you! Just be creative, think out of the box, keep it sexy and intriguing!

If you'd like to join the Royal family, send us the first 15K words (60 pages) of your completed manuscript to submissions@royaltypublishinghouse.com

# LIKE OUR PAGE!

Be sure to LIKE our Royalty Publishing House page on Facebook!

CPSIA information can be obtained
at www.ICGtesting.com
Printed in the USA
LVHW091624200619
621865LV00005B/858/P